Addicted to My Homegirl's Husband 2

A novel by
Lady Lissa
&
Shelli Marie

D1519391

Where We Left Off...

Rachel Gwinn

What the hell? I hadn't heard from Quinton since the conversation we had before he left for his trip, and that was over a month ago. I still couldn't believe that he told me the two of us weren't in a relationship. This whole time I was thinking he was my man.

Well, he sure let me know he wasn't nothing but my damn friend. A friend that had been missing in action, just like my other one.

All this time... no word from Quinton. There was no word from Justice either. The only two people that meant something to me besides my mother.

Since Justice's number was no longer in service, finding her was a dead end. Then there were the cops who I couldn't run to anymore. Orders of Quinton Marshall. What the hell?

Why should I be even obeying his orders when he wasn't even answering my calls or responding to my text messages? It was like he had me blocked or something. Why would he do that?

This nigga had put me in my own apartment and furnished it, and for what? Payment for the dude I popped for him? That wasn't shit and I would do it ten times over if it would make him commit to me...

That was something Quinton hadn't seemed too interested in since he moved me up out of my mama's house. While I thought he did it for us to spend more time together, it had been just the opposite.

Like I told him, if he was going to stay away, he should have left me in my mom's place. At least then, I wouldn't be lonely every day and night like I had been the past couple of months.

Right now, I was living in an apartment by my damn self. Now if I invited another nigga over here, he would have some shit to say about it.

That got me thinking. Maybe I should invite another dude to my place to sit on the furniture that Quinton had bought for me. I wouldn't sleep with him though because I didn't want to make my bae mad at me and mess up things between us for good. No, that may not have been a good idea. The consequences would be much too great.

If Quinton left me alone forever, my heart would be broken beyond repair. Sadly, I could get over losing the material things, but I couldn't get over losing him...

As I sat there going through every emotion known to man, I eventually calmed down when I realized that it didn't matter what Quinton said. We were together. He was my man, and I was his woman and just as soon as I saw him, I would make that shit clear to him.

But where was he? Did something happen to him while he was on vacation? Did he ever return? Better yet where was Justice?

Two people missing and nobody knew where they were, and nobody done heard from them. That shit was insane. It almost felt like God was punishing me for something.

"Where is this nigga?" I huffed and dialed Quinton.

Of course, he didn't answer, but it didn't stop me from trying. Shit, I was still keeping hope alive, but it was driving me insane not to speak to him.

At this point, I was almost desperate enough to call Shawn and ask him if he knew what was going on with Quinton. The only reason I hadn't hit him up was because of how we left things when we saw each other the night at the club.

As my frustrations flared up again, I wished that I had someone to talk to. Namely, Justice.

Her eighteenth birthday was coming up the following month, but I was convinced that she would never celebrate it. Why? Because I was actually starting to believe that my best friend was dead and that I'd never see her again.

No matter how hard I tried, I couldn't keep the faith that I once had. The longer Justice had been missing, the more that the hope to find her faded, until it fully disappeared...

With Quinton, it was a different story. I had a pretty good feeling that his ass was alive and kicking.

Reason being, I kept checking Quinton's page every other day, and nothing had changed until today. He had changed his status from single to not only in a relationship but married!

"What in the actual fuck!" I stressed. "When the fuck did he get married?"

As I scrolled on his page looking for information about his marriage, I saw a pair of hands, a man's, and female's, both with wedding rings.

"Oh my God! Quinton got married!" I yelled as I paced the floor of my apartment. "Who the fuck did he marry?"

To try to figure this shit out, I studied the female's hand to see if I recognized it, but I didn't. The fingernails were freshly manicured and beautiful as hell.

That didn't much matter though if the bitch couldn't ball that muthafucka up and swing back when I came for her. Oh, because I was coming for her. Just as soon as I found out who she was...

KNOCK! KNOCK! KNOCK!

My body jumped from the unexpected pounding at my door. I had no idea who it was, but I wasn't in the mood. Not when I was on the verge of tears. So, unless it was Quinton on the other side of that door, I didn't want to see anybody else.

With anxiety rushing through me, I marched over to the door and pulled it back. When I did, I got the shock of my damn life.

"JUSTICE! JUSTICE IS IT REALLY YOU?!!" I asked as I grabbed my best friend and wrapped my arms around her.

Tears streamed from my eyes as I held her tight. I didn't think I'd ever see her again. Where the hell had she been all this time? I had so many questions for her!

"Yes, it's really me!"

"Where the heck have you been? Are you okay? Were you being held captive?" I asked. "I'm sorry to be asking so many questions but I was really worried about you. Me and mama both were."

"I'm sorry I worried y'all. I never meant to," she apologized with a smile.

Justice's skin was glowing and there was something different about her. The way she dressed, her hair and the way she carried herself. If she was kidnapped, she must've been held captive by a fucking prince!

"Come and sit down," I urged as was finally able to take my eyes off of her and shut the door. "How did you get here?"

"I took an Uber."

"An Uber? Where have you been? Tell me everything," I questioned as I sat next to her on the sofa ready to hear each and every detail of what happened to her.

"You won't believe me when I tell you. I can barely believe any of it myself."

"Shoot, you've been gone for two months, so try me."

"Well, after I found my mom's body..."

"You found your mom?" I asked in surprise.

"Yea, after I left from your mom's place and went home. She was there. Shot. Dead..."

"Wow! I had no idea. That must have been so hard for you."

"It was, but I know that she's in a better place now. My mom led a pretty wild life with all the drugs and stuff..." Justice took a deep breath and brushed a tear away.

My mouth hit the floor when I saw the rings on her finger. Like those were the same fingernails and rings I saw in Quinton's story and on his page. What the hell?

"Uhm Justice, did you get married?"

"Uh yea. See what had happened was…"

"Bitch you married Quinton!" I shrieked.

No fucking way had that muthafucka gone out and married my best friend behind my back. No fucking way!

This whole time he knew that I was looking for her, and he knew where she was! THE WHOLE FUCKING TIME!!

Chapter One

Justice Patterson

"Uhm Justice, did you get married?"

"Uh yea. See what had happened was..."

"Bitch you married Quinton!"

"Huh?" I asked, confused as to how she would know I married Quinton.

As Rachel grabbed my ring finger and pointed to the huge wedding set on my left hand, she asked, "you married Quinton Marshall, didn't you?"

"How did you know that? I mean, that Quinton is my husband."

After Rachel quickly went through her phone, she turned the picture towards me and shoved it in my face. This chick was acting weird.

"He posted this on his Facebook page!" she yelled. She seemed really upset, and I didn't understand why. "You're wearing the same rings as the one in this picture! You gonna tell me that ain't your hand when you're wearing the same damn polish and everything!"

"I didn't say it wasn't mine, but where is all this hostility coming from?" I questioned.

Rachel was like a defense attorney cross examining a witness. Like what the fuck did I do to deserve that?

The only thing that came to mind was that Rachel was being salty because I married Quinton when I couldn't even stand his ass not that long ago. What she didn't know was that I still suspected that he had something to do with my mom's murder, so that old saying, 'Keep your friends close and your enemies closer' was exactly what I was doing with my husband.

Even though Quinton swore he had nothing to do with it, I still had my suspicious, and I didn't care how long it took, I was going to find out the truth. And may the Lord help him if he did have my mom killed because he would definitely have some shit on his hands.

"You don't think I have a right to be hostile?" Rachel asked as she eyed me down.

"Not this hostile."

"Where the hell have you been, Justice? How did you know where I lived? Were you with Quinton this entire time? Why didn't you call me? Do you know how fucking worried I was?"

"Can you slow down with the questions so I can speak?"

"Speak," she said as she spread her arms and sat down. She crossed her arms over her chest and rocked back and forth… a move she often did when she was angry.

"Well for starters, when I tried to call you, I found out that your number had been changed…"

"Well, you got yours changed first, girl! Do you know how many times I dialed that number trying to reach you? I called even after it was disconnected, hoping that one day it would be back on, and you would answer. I just needed to know that you were okay! I missed you so much, Justice. To be honest, I thought you were dead! Especially after we found out what happened to your mom!" she explained.

Okay, now I understood why she was hostile. I had been gone for two months without any contact whatsoever, but that wasn't my idea. If it would have been up to me, I would have contacted her the same day I left. Of course, Quinton had other plans for me.

"I'm so sorry, Rachel. I tried to call you, but like I said, your number had changed. That's why when I got up this morning, I caught an Uber straight to your mom's house. When you or Ms. Nancy didn't answer the door, your neighbor Ms. Leslie popped out of her place and took it upon herself to tell me all of your business girl!" I laughed then thought about it. "Wait, you don't think she'll go telling folks that I'm back or that I'm at your apartment, do you?"

"Fuck her! I wanna know where the hell you been and how the fuck you ended up marrying

Quinton! Quinton, of all people Justice! Really! What were you thinking?"

The way Rachel was acting all hysterical about me being missing for months without so much as a word, you would think she would be happier to see me. Instead, she was standing here freaking out because I got married. I guess I could understand her shock about my marriage to Quinton, but why would she act that way when it was her who defended him when I thought he was a bad guy? That shit had me totally baffled.

"Why you keep coming at me so aggressively? I feel like I'm being attacked for some reason. What is going on with you Rachel?" I asked.

While I understood why she was a bit hostile when I first walked in, her attitude right now was a bit much. No matter how shocked she was to see me or how worried she was while I was gone, I did not deserve this treatment from her.

"For some reason, I just thought you would be happier to see me..."

"Are you fucking serious right now, Justice?" Rachel questioned once more with tears filling her eyes.

As the clear liquid began to leak down her cheeks, my best friend hugged me again. When she released me, she wiped her face and forced a smile. I was so confused right now. How did we go from her hollering at me to her sobbing and now grinning? It was like she was on an emotional rollercoaster. What the hell was really going on?

"Why are crying, Rachel? I know I was gone a long time without calling, but I was scared. First seeing my mother lying there dead and then worrying about being caught up in the foster care system. It just all happened so fast. The only thing I could of to do was run. I know you're mad at me, but I hope you can understand why I did what I did."

"How can I be mad at you when you're standing here well and alive? I'm trippin' and I owe you an apology because of how I acted when you first got here. I didn't mean to lash out at you, but make no mistake about it, I am super happy that you're here," Rachel answered with a nervous grin.

Sure, I heard what she said, and I actually believed it when she said she was happy to see me. But still, I got the feeling that something was off.

Before I could ask her about it, Quinton was ringing my phone. When I didn't pick up the first time, he called right back, and I was forced to answer. If I didn't, I knew he would be worried.

"Hello?"

"Justice? Where'd you go, baby? I woke up and you were gone. You left without even saying a word. Do you know how worried I've been? Now you got me driving all around town looking for you."

"Sorry, I didn't mean to worry you. You were sleeping so peacefully, and I didn't wanna wake you."

"Justice, you know you could've woken me up. I would've taken you wherever you needed to go."

"Quinton, it wasn't that big of a deal. I just caught an Uber," I explained.

The change in Rachel's posture when I mentioned Quinton's name was weird as hell. I didn't know what her problem was with him, but considering he was my husband, and she was my best friend, they would have to learn to get along.

"I thought you took one of the cars since you know how to drive now." Quinton teased.

"Just because I know how to drive doesn't make it legal. You still need to take me to get my license. I'm ready to go when you are," I said.

"You are?"

"Yes! After all the driving you had me doing on the freeway, and how I got us home safely... I'm sure I can pass that driver's test with ease."

"Justice, you know how to drive?" Rachel blurted out.

"Yes, I do and I'm pretty good at it too!" I bragged proudly.

"Who are you talking to?" Quinton asked anxiously. "Where are you?"

"I'm over at Rachel's…"

"What the hell? Are you really out in the hood when you know it ain't safe?" Quinton asked with concern etched in his tone.

"I'll be legal in a couple of weeks. Besides, you know I got that ID!"

"What ID?" Rachel gasped and narrowed her eyes as she stared me down.

"Look, I know Rachel is your homegirl and y'all ain't seen each other for a minute, but I need you to come home. You can come back to visit when it's safe."

Quinton was so overprotective. It was cute, yet annoying at times.

"What? Why I gotta go now?" I asked.

"Because I said so babe. I just told you it isn't safe for you out there. Tell your friend that you will see her some other time, but right now, I'm on my way to get you."

"But Quinton, you don't even know where I am. Rachel doesn't live with her mama no more. She got her own crib and everything!"

"Justice, I hear what you're saying, but right now, I need to come pick you up. Send me the address and I'll be there shortly."

"What's the rush? I'm here now, so I just wanted to visit with my friend. It's been a couple of months since we saw each other, and I missed her."

"The rush is that I'm worried about you. Plus, you left so early that you ruined the surprise I had for you."

"Surprise?" I gasped and then grinned while sending him Rachel's address.

"Yes, a surprise. Now, be ready when I get there. I'm right down the street," he stated.

"You're on this side already?" I questioned knowing that we lived far from the hood.

"Yea, you don't think I panicked when I realized you were gone! Shit, I didn't even wait for my cell to charge. I just snatched it up and threw it on this slow ass charger I got in my car. Soon as that green light went to flashing and my phone powered on, best believe I was calling to see where my wife was at."

"Your wife, huh?" I giggled. "I gotta get used to you saying that shit."

"Well, get used to it because I ain't goin' nowhere. Now, be ready. I'm down the street."

By the tone of Quinton's voice, I knew that he was serious about me leaving. As badly as I wanted to stay over at Rachel's house and catch her up on everything that had happened over the last couple of months, now wasn't the right time.

"Okay, I'll be ready. Let me know when you're outside," I said as I continued to hold the phone up to my ear.

"Wait, you're leaving already! You just got here!" Rachel stressed.

"I know sis, and I wanted to spend time with you, but Quinton needs me to come home. Don't worry though. I'll either be back later on today or tomorrow."

"Well, what kind of shit is that? Now that you're married, you can't go and come as you please! That nigga got you on a time limit or some shit! You just got here and I ain't seen or heard from my BEST FRIEND in months! Just because he decided to settle down suddenly..."

"Hush, Rachel." I laughed and cut her off. "You know what I mean."

It was apparent that Quinton didn't see the humor in it because soon as Rachel said it, he started grumbling. "Shit funny, huh?"

"And you know what I mean too," I repeated myself calmly.

"Just as long as you remember that you're married now," he stated.

"How the hell can I forget with this big ass rock on my finger?" I laughed. "Or the small ceremony you set up! Or the honeymoon suite you got for us..."

"Oh God! Y'all fucked?" Rachel gasped.

Once again, my best friend was on the brink of having a crying fit as I briefly described the day that

Quinton and I were married. By then I was finished, I was in tears too.

"Are you over there crying?" my husband teased.

"Stop it, Quinton. You know how emotional I've been lately," I replied.

"Wait, I wanna hear all about what was going on while you were missing, Justice. Were you with Quinton the whole time?" Rachel probed.

"You can call and tell her whatever she wants to know another time, but right now, I'm pulling up. Come on outside, baby."

"I'll be right out," I said as I hung the phone up.

When I turned around to give Rachel a hug and tell her bye, she was staring at me with fire in her eyes. The vibe around her was so intense that I immediately became defensive.

This chick was at it again. Her and her wildly uncontrollable emotions were confusing the hell out of me.

"What? I told you I'm gonna come back, boo."

"Seriously, Justice?"

"Yes, I am."

"I can't believe this shit! You really just gonna show up outta nowhere and then run up outta here just as fast? I have my own place now. Tell that nigga you wanna stay, and you'll get an Uber home later."

"Rachel, stop it. We just went through this. I'm good and I'm gonna come back." I replied as peacefully as possible and went to hug her anyway.

As I wrapped my arms around her, I instantly felt her body tense up. To calm her, I squeezed tighter.

"You know you're my best friend and I love you, girl.

"If you love me, you won't let nothing come between us, Justice."

"Nothing will ever come between us, Rachel."

"You promise?"

"I promise."

"Not even Quinton?"

Where was this line of questioning coming from? What the hell was her problem?

At one time, she was Quinton's biggest supporter. Now, it was like she didn't want me to have anything to do with him. I couldn't understand was going on with Rachel.

"Girl, you are seriously trippin'. My friendship with you has nothing to do with my marriage to Quinton. Just because I'm married, doesn't mean things between us will change. You will always be my homegirl and best friend."

After giving Rachel one last hug and promising to call her later, I rushed to the door and opened it because now Quinton was blowing up my cell. I knew that if I didn't hurry and come out, he would be at the damn door knocking and ringing the bell.

"You better call me!" Rachel hollered out as I ran down the pathway leading to the parking lot where my husband was waiting on me.

Upon approaching the truck, I stared at Quinton who was sitting behind the wheel looking fine as ever. His facial hair was always trimmed to perfection and those eyes... those seductive slanted eyes. The way that he used them to look at me always melted my insides. Like damn!

Although the sight of Quinton always caused my heart to skip an extra beat, in the back of my mind, I still moved with caution. How could I not?

As I slowly fell harder for Quinton, it became more difficult to keep the wall around my heart up. Honestly, all I wanted was the truth and until I got it, I would continue to tread with caution. That was exactly why I left the house without telling him.

A lot of good that did me because those couple of hours that I thought I was going to spend with Rachel got smooth cut off. It was really disappointing because I was anxious to visit with my friend.

It was the first time being out of the house alone since I arrived at the home that I now shared with my husband. Also, I was excited to finally get a moment to myself. We had been back from Vegas for a month, and I was still trapped in the house. As beautiful as it was, I was tired being there.

Of course, that didn't quite work out the way I planned. Not even close.

"Sorry about that." I smiled as I climbed into the passenger side of Quinton's truck.

"You ain't gotta be sorry, Justice. I understand your need to see your friend, but now is just not the time. You only have a few weeks before you turn eighteen. After that, you can be out as much as you want to, and you won't hear shit from me. Right now, you can't just be running out without letting me know where you are. How the hell can I protect you if I don't know where you are?"

"You're right Quinton, and that's why I'm sorry. I should've told you I was leaving and where I would be. I didn't mean to worry you," I apologized and patted his hand.

Sadly, affection had barely been present in our unplanned marriage. A few pecks and hugs here and there, but honestly, the closest we got to intimacy was the kiss at our ceremony. That lip lock right there had me wanting to go back to our suite and let Quinton rock my world. Only that shit didn't happen.

That night we both passed out with all of our clothes on. That was how drunk we were. The next morning, it was time to shower, get dressed and hit the road.

Once we made it back from our trip, Quinton went back to hugging the block for several hours a day, almost every day. Sometimes, like today, he was really exhausted. That was why I didn't wake him.

"I just figured you were tired and wouldn't feel like taking me anywhere," I confessed.

"Shit, this ain't new. I done hustled the block three days straight before I stopped to sleep," Quinton explained as we hopped on the highway. "That's why you left, huh?"

"Yea, I thought you would be asleep all day and I didn't wanna disturb you."

"Naw, you thought I was gonna sweat you for some of those goodies since we're married now," he teased with a smile.

"Trust, I wasn't worried about that. You made it perfectly clear that you wanted to wait until my birthday. I'm cool with that." I laughed and got anxious just thinking about getting sexed down for the first time.

"That don't mean we can't cuddle."

"You know what cuddling leads to. We found that shit out the other night when your... ah... your... ah," I stuttered as I searched for the proper terminology to use.

"When my dick stood up?" Quinton laughed. "Shit, that happens every time I'm around you, wifey. Real talk."

"Hush," I said as I blushed and giggled.

"No, but seriously, Justice. My room is your room too. We're married."

"I know."

"Well, why you ain't you came in there?"

"I just didn't feel comfortable just coming in there and climbing in your bed without an invitation."

"You're my wife. You don't need a damn invitation."

"Well, even though we are married, it really doesn't feel like it," I admitted. "It seemed more like a dream. Maybe because I was intoxicated."

"So, you wouldn't have married me if you weren't drunk?"

"Well, it ain't like you ever told me you loved me or no shit like that. We hadn't even kissed before we were pronounced husband and wife. And we definitely ain't fucked..."

"Wait a minute... if... no, *when*, I put my dick in you, it ain't gonna be no fucking going on. I'm gonna make love to my wife."

"Whaaaat?" I clowned and bounced in my seat laughing.

"I'm serious and I'm more serious abou waiting until you turn eighteen and become legal. That fake ID shit don't make you grown."

"That fake ID don't make our marriage valid either, but I ain't said shit about that."

"Everything is real on your ID except your birthday, so don't think you don't belong to me." Quinton chuckled but I didn't take it like that.

Was he being funny, or did he really think of me as if I was a piece of fucking property? This shit wasn't going to work if that was what he was thinking.

Not wasting another moment, I called Quinton on his remark. "Uhm, what do you mean I belong to you? Just because we're married doesn't make me your property. Nobody owns me!" I stated.

"I didn't mean it like that," he refined.

"Well, that's how you said it."

"Damn, you feisty!"

"Just know that I'm not gonna take no shit from you or anybody else just because a piece of fucking paper says that we're married."

"I hear you babe, and I didn't mean it that way. I'm sorry if it came out that way, but I ain't never had no wife before. I'm still learning my duties as a husband," he confessed.

Quinton may have looked at me as a young chick because he had seven years on me, but he

e if he were to underestimate my level
ts. With him, I wasn't about to bullshit.
n person, and not anyone's damn

"Don't be sitting over there mad because you took shit the wrong way. I said I ain't mean it like that."

"Long as you know shit ain't about to go like that, we good," I replied as I quickly calmed down.

"Good, because my surprise would've been fucked up if we got home and you were in bad mood and shit."

Home? Damn. I couldn't believe that Quinton's home was now my home.

Things were moving too fast for me. Way too fast.

Hell, I wasn't even eighteen yet and here I was wearing a wedding ring. Married to Quinton Marshall at that.

Who would've thought?

Chapter Two

Quinton Marshall

After Justice and I got back from Vegas, I had spent the entire of month keeping her away from everyone. It was all going great until this one particular day.

When I came out of my room that morning to look for my wife and found her gone, I shot to the hood where I knew she would be. I knew she had been itching to visit Rachel ever since we got back, but every time that she brought it up, I had an excuse as to why it wasn't safe for her to go over there just yet. Hell, the last thing I needed the two of them doing was chit chatting. Seeing that I had moved her into her own spot, I assumed that it would take Justice much longer to find her than it actually did.

The more I thought about it, the faster I sped down the freeway. I had to get to Justice before Rachel had the chance to start running her mouth about us.

As I veered off the highway and took the main road to get to the hood, anxiety managed to strike me with enough force to place fear within me. It was a foreign feeling and also a sign of weakness, so I did everything that I could to shake it off. I had to.

Hell, I was known as a kingpin in these streets. What the hell did I look like chasing down a female? It was bad enough that I had tricked Justice into marrying me.

All the unexplainable things that I had been doing was way out of character for me. But why? Why now?

Shit, was a nigga falling in love? Did I really care for Justice more than I was willing to admit?

"No, nigga!" I chanted to myself. What I needed to do was calm down.

The main thing that bothered me was the fact that I hadn't gotten the chance to come clean to both of them. For now, I needed them separated until I had the opportunity to do so.

But damn. How was I going to do that shit? It wasn't like I had planned all of this.

"You tell Rachel you got married, huh?" I probed soon as Justice stopped talking shit on the way back to the house.

While she was going off about her not being a piece of property, I was trying to get answers of my own. I really needed to know how much her friend blabbed before I spilled any of the truth just yet.

"Yea, Q, I told her that I got married, but before I could tell her who my husband was, she saw my ring then put two and two together."

"What you mean?"

"I mean that Rachel already knew that you were married because apparently you posted a pic of our hands on social media. She just didn't know it was me until she saw the rings on my hand."

"I didn't know she followed me like that," I lied. Man, I wanted to kick myself for doing that shit.

Maybe I should've thought twice before I posted the pic and announced our marriage. But then again, I needed everyone to know that I was no longer on the market. That meant I wasn't going to be fucking all these hoes anymore.

"I didn't know she followed you either Quinton, but I sure found out today!"

"So, I take it Rachel tripped out when she found out it was you that I married, huh?" I asked Justice.

"Honestly, Rachel tripped about everything that I told her..."

"Everything! What all did you tell her?" I asked growing nervous again.

"I mean, I didn't go into all the details of where I've been if that's what you're worried about. I didn't really have the chance to tell her much before you called and said you were coming to scoop me up. I just think she was in shock about everything. She was whooping and hollering so much that at one point, I swear that I thought I was gonna have to fight her."

"Fight her? For what?" I questioned in a panic.

"Of course, I wasn't going to physically fight her! She's my best friend, but you should've seen the way she was looking at me when she talked about me running off with you. It's like she thought I did something to purposely hurt her or something. The way her eyes shot daggers at me as she fired question after question..."

"Questions like what?"

"Like where I've been all this time. Did I know about my mom's passing. Do I know who killed her. Was I with you the whole time. Just all kind of shit!"

"Damn, yo homegirl nosy as fuck! What did you tell her?"

"I couldn't tell her anything because as soon as we started talking about it, you texted to tell me that you were outside," Justice explained.

"Well, if you didn't tell her shit, why was she so mad?"

"Because she wanted to know everything, and I didn't get a chance to tell her anything."

"What did you wanna tell her?" I pressed.

"I at least wanted to brag about how you rescued me. I don't know what I would've done without you."

Justice's words tugged at a nigga's heart, and I felt myself get a little emotional. To dodge the unwanted sensitivity, I had to get comical.

"Oh, I rescued you, huh? Like a knight in shining armor or some shit?" I teased as we finally made it to the long rocky road that led to our home.

"Seriously, Quinton. If I haven't thanked you enough, thanks again."

"You're my wife and we're beyond..."

"You don't have to keep reminding me that I'm your wife, Q. I think about it every time I look down at this incredibly large diamond that practically takes up my whole darn finger."

"You don't like it? Is it too big?"

"Oh, no, it fits. I was just referring to the size of the stone," Justice replied with a sigh.

"What's wrong then?" I asked.

"You want me to be honest, Q?"

"No doubt, baby. Always."

"Okay... I know I already said this, but... well... ah... other than this ring, I don't really feel like I'm married."

"You really don't, huh?" I checked as I pulled up to the house, parked and went around to her side to open the door for her.

"No, not really."

"Well, this may make you feel more like my wife." I smiled as we went into the house, and I escorted my new bride up to the master bedroom where I had moved all of her things.

Oddly, my surprise didn't seem to faze her. If it did, she sure wasn't smiling. Instead of her being happy about the move into my room and all the new shit I bought for her, Justice wanted to call Rachel.

"I can't believe that I rushed up outta there and didn't leave my new number or get hers," she whined.

"Can't you call her mother and get her number?" I asked knowing that Justice had just gotten a new phone and her contacts hadn't transferred over from the old broken one.

"My other phone won't power on at all, so I can't get any numbers out of it."

"Look, you can wait a few weeks..."

"No! Can you just please go by there and get it for me when you go back to that side?" Justice pleaded.

"Yep, I gotta go over there later on tonight. I'll swing by if it ain't too late."

"Please leave a little early if you have to. I really wanna talk to her. I think she's kind of mad at me and I would be too. Look how long I went without calling her. She thought that I was dead. Damn, I just feel so bad, Quinton."

"Aight, I gotcha," I assured. "Let me go downstairs and make some calls. That way, I can leave in a few."

"Okay, while you're doing that, I'm gonna go make some wings and fries. You want some?"

"You know I do." I smiled as we walked out of the master bedroom and descended the stairs.

While Justice went off to the kitchen, I went to the bonus room and closed myself in for privacy. First thing I needed to do was find out what Rachel was up to. Since I had her blocked, she hadn't been able to call or leave messages.

That wasn't such a good thing right now because without hearing from her, I didn't know what she was thinking or plotting to do. Luckily, she didn't know where I lived and for now, she didn't know Justice's number. Those were my only two advantages, and I didn't know how long I could hold onto either of them.

"Let me go ahead and call Rachel before Justice gets ahold of Ms. Nancy and gets her fuckin' number," I whispered to myself.

After getting up and locking the door, I dialed Rachel's phone. When she answered on the first ring, it didn't shock me at all.

"What the fuck, Q?" Rachel cried as soon as she picked up. "You really kidnapped my friend and forced her to marry you? I thought me and you had something going! What the fuck were you thinking?"

"Whoa! Whoa! Whoa! First of all, I done told you that the shit was over between me, and you before I even made a move with Justice..."

"So, you fucked her?"

All that yelling and crying was starting to make my head hurt. What was Rachel even talking about?

"Look, why are you trippin'? It ain't even that serious!" I stated.

"Of course, you would say that since you have no fucking feelings whatsoever!"

"I do have feelings," I hissed.

"Shit, you sure don't have any for me! I am in love with you, and what did you do? You went and married my homegirl, so that makes you my homegirl's husband! And you know what that makes me? Stupid!"

"You ain't stupid Rachel!"

"I feel stupid is fuck yo! I can't believe you really married Justice, especially knowing that she's my best fucking friend in the whole world. You know how I feel about you, so I feel like you married her to hurt me!"

"Get this, nothing concerning me, and Justice was to hurt you. To be honest, when I married her, I didn't even think about you... at all! So, you can put that shit to rest," I stated firmly.

Shit, I wasn't lying about that either. I married Justice for my own selfish reasons. None of that shit had anything to do with Rachel. I was shocked that she would even think my relationship with Justice had anything to do with her. That was some wild shit!

"How did you get her to agree to marry you in the first place? You had to have tricked her into saying yes because she didn't even like your ass!" Rachel admitted.

"Well, she likes me now," I teased. "She likes me a lot."

Shamelessly, I could admit that I was trying to get under her skin. Why was I trying to do that? Because she was trying to do the same to me. Yes, it was childish, but fuck it.

"What did you say?" Rachel badgered.

"What you mean what did I say?"

"I mean you had to say something to get her to agree to do that..."

"I didn't have to say shit. We just spent time with each other and kinda fell for one another. It wasn't planned or no shit like that..."

"So, you love her, Q? Is that what you're saying to me?" she asked. I could hear the whining in her voice as she spoke.

"Rachel, cut that shit out. I told you before I even went on the trip..."

"You had Justice with you way before then, Q. She ran off with you the same fucking day that her mother was killed. Come to think of it, it was her voice that I heard in the background that day you butt dialed me!" she shrieked. "I can't believe you right now!"

"Yo you trippin'!"

"I find it very hard to believe that you had a woman with you before you left town, only to come back married to Justice. Believe me when I say that I know how to add shit up nigga! I can put two and two together just like the next bitch! Lemme ask you something though..."

"What's that?"

"Justice said you helped her after her mom was killed. Real talk... do you know anything about that shit?" she interrogated like she was ready to go to the cops with what she thought she knew.

That wouldn't be the smartest thing for her to do seeing as how the last person that threatened me was nothing but a bunch of ashes now. This bitch should know better.

"That street business is a dangerous one to get wrapped up in. It's okay to question me because we know each other but ask the wrong person and the results may be different."

"Different how?" Rachel inquired.

"You know exactly what the fuck I'm saying to you," I pressed.

"Are you threatening me Q?"

"You and I both know that I don't do threats. I do, however, make promises because I keep that shit. You know how it goes out there in these streets when folks go poking around about shit that don't concern them, so step lightly," I warned.

"I'm not about to play with you, Q, but you got some explaining to do."

"Look, the only people I owe any explanations to are the man upstairs and my fuckin' wife! I don't owe you a muthafuckin' thing! What I will tell you is that I will be letting Justice know that I used to mess around with you. It was before I got married to her, so I'm sure she won't trip..."

"Oh, when it comes from my mouth, I'm sure she's gonna trip!" Rachel responded as if she was irritated. Hell, I didn't understand why she was irritated, especially when she was the one causing all the fucking problems.

"That's cool because like I said twice before, it was in the past," I repeated. "Just know that I'll never fuck with or talk to you again if you go running to my wife..."

"Your wife?!" Rachel shrieked. "How dare you say that to me after all we've been through. I've killed for you and would do it again if I had to. Has Justice earned anything?"

"She's earned my trust..."

"And your love?" Rachel pressed. "Tell me, why is she so special that you would want to marry her over me?"

"The little shit between me and you was nothing more than a few thank you fucks for having a nigga's back and murking a muthafucka for me, Rachel." I reminded. "You wanna join that dead muthafucka?"

"Ah, no."

"You always making shit more than it really is. Just let that shit go and keep your fuckin' mouth closed until I have a chance to tell Justice in my own way."

"You would really have me killed behind all this shit when you're the one who not only ran off with my best friend, but you fucking married her, Q?"

I didn't have any more time for this shit! Rachel was making this harder than it had to be. Just let the shit go and move the fuck on!

"I'm about to go..."

"So, that's it? That's all?" Rachel whined. "What am I supposed to do now that you put me in this damn apartment knowing that I can't afford the rent?"

"The money I paid will have you good there for the next four and a half months or so. After that, renew the six month lease and start paying full rent..."

"How?"

"Get a job or hustle for me."

"Work for you?" Rachel sighed heavily then smacked her lips like she was annoyed.

"Yes, get this paper."

There was a brief pause in the conversation before Rachel started talking again. "So, if I work for you, I'll be able to call your phone and see you too?"

Was this chick serious? Was she still trying to push up on me when she knew that I was married to her best friend?

Now, I was starting to question shit. "I thought you were really loyal."

"Why are you doubting it?"

"Because you act like you still wanna get at a nigga after I done told you that I'm married to Justice. You think that I'm going to jeopardize my marriage to keep fucking with you?"

Just like before, there was a momentary silence, and the conversation was brought to another halt. While Rachel was thinking of how to respond, I was wondering why Shawn had called me for the third time in a row.

"Business, Q. You made it perfectly clear that there was nothing but business between us," she responded. "I can stick to that, just let me know who I'll be working under. Ah, unless that would be you."

"I'm gonna put you under Shawn. That's him calling me on the other line. Let me see what's up with his ass and I'll either call you or have him call you."

All of a sudden, this bitch went from mad and irritated to cheery and joyful. Was it because she was about to make some serious money? Or was it because she was going to work up under Shawn?

For Rachel's sake, it better had been the first one. If it wasn't and she thought she was about to fool with my boy to make me jealous, she was going to inherit an ass whooping along with it. Doreen didn't play that shit.

"Yo," I said when I finally answered Shawn's call.

"Nigga, why you ain't been pickin' up yo fucking phone?" he questioned.

"Nigga, I'm out here handling business. You been blowing my phone up like you my bitch! What's the fuckin' emergency?!"

"Yo, that bitch came over to my crib with the heater, man! She shot my door up and everything."

The more Shawn told me about all that shit, the more pissed I became at his baby mama for going over there acting a fool like that. All that changed in a blink of an eye though.

Once he confessed to having Syanna watch their daughter, I couldn't even be mad at Doreen no more. That was a fucked- up move and he was the dumb one.

"You good though, right?"

"Yea, but now she said she ain't gonna let me see my daughter no more."

"Don't sweat that shit bro! That ain't gonna last long. She gon be calling you cuz she gon be needing something. I bet she let you see Laya then, playa," I clowned.

"You may be right, Q, but Doreen stubborn as fuck though."

"Well, I know what I'm talking about. I ain't the boss for nothing. I got experience in this shit." I laughed.

"Aight, BOSS! How was your trip?" Shawn inquired. "I'm assuming you're back because you're finally answering your phone."

"Nigga I been back a month. I know Peep and Jon done told you I been dippin' in and out of the hood every night. We just been missing each other. When you go hit the block, I be on my way back home."

"Them niggas ain't said shit the about that. I been tryna get ahold of you, Q," Shawn complained. "You ain't answered yo line for shit."

"It was crunch- time, nigga! All my dough was turned in on time, so if y'all wasn't calling me for business, I wasn't answering shit," I told him.

"How you know it wasn't about business?"

"Shawn, did you once hit my cell with the code?"

"No…"

"Well, there was no reason to stop what I was doing to answer or hit you back. That's the problem with y'all. Y'all let the drama get in the way of business. Calling me every time Doreen wanna act a fool ain't reason enough for me to answer my damn phone. I got my own personal shit to deal with. Plus, you knew how Doreen was before you knocked that her up."

"You right, Q." Shawn sounded like he felt bad for handling me that way. It was cool though. I knew how that shit went. "My bad."

"No fucking worries, man. I'm back and the trip was good. Matter of fact, it was real good," I boasted and told him all about Vegas while purposely leaving out the part about me getting married.

That nigga didn't need to know all that shit. Not just yet, anyway…

Chapter Three

Shawn Fulcher

Finally, Quinton was answering his phone after ignoring my calls for nearly a month. Even though he was back to checking his traps, I didn't know shit about it.

Why was all of them niggas leaving me out the loop? What the fuck did I do?

While I was in the hood overseeing Quinton's hardheaded ass workers, ain't none of them little niggas said shit about him being back in town. They damn sure didn't mention that there was any tension in the camp.

Then to top it off, Quinton wanted to put another person up under me. A bitch I couldn't stand at that... Rachel!

Man, this shit was fucked up because even if it wasn't a conspiracy, it sure as hell felt like it. For sho'.

There I was, left to look after the misfits only to get treated like an outsider as soon as I couldn't control them. Fucking around with dudes that didn't listen for shit.

"That's just how I got caught up!" I fussed thinking about how I had to leave my crib to check on Jimmy. Couldn't even leave that cat in charge for a few hours without my world being turned upside down.

After filling Quinton in about everything that happened while he was out of touch, we ended the call. Now, I had to figure out a way to deal with my baby mama since she had been keeping my shorty from me for the past five weeks. I had been calling Doreen nearly every day to see my baby girl, but each time I did, she refused. To sweeten the deal and make up for letting Syanna watch Laya, I had even shown up at her place with flowers, bought her a couple of designer handbags and brought her dinner from her favorite restaurants. When that shit didn't work, I didn't know what else to do to get her to change her mind.

At this point, it wasn't even about me or how I felt. It was about our baby girl and how much I knew she missed her dad.

Laya was used to seeing me two or three times a week and every other weekend. We both looked forward to that shit and now Doreen wanted to use her authority to keep us apart. All because she was salty.

No matter how much she tried to convince me it was all behind Syanna babysitting our daughter, I knew better. This chick was angrier about catching my dick in the girl's mouth than she was about anything else.

Well, Doreen should've thought about that shit before she wanted to call it quits. What did she think? That she could break up with me and still control who I fucked with? Nope, not going to happen.

If she didn't let up soon, I was even thinking about threatening her. I had rights as a father, and I had signed the birth certificate. That alone would get me visitation.

Doreen was damn lucky I didn't mess around with the law like that. People with badges in my line of work was off limits. That was what gave my baby mama the upper hand in this particular case.

Ugh, this chick was about to drive me crazy. If it wasn't Doreen, it was Syanna. She just wouldn't leave me the hell alone. After all the shit that had gone down between us, you would think that she wouldn't wanna fuck with me anymore, but that bitch was just as crazy as my baby mama. Between those two, I didn't know which one was worse. All I knew was that I was ready to quit both their asses.

Maybe it was time for me to get a new friend. These old bitches had been way more trouble than I bargained for.

"I should just step out tonight and look for the next bitch," I thought aloud.

To get somebody to roll to the club with me that night, I hit up my boy Miguel. When he said he was down, I told him I'd scoop him up in a couple of hours.

Once I hung the phone up, I headed to the bathroom to wash my ass. Soon as I finished and got out to dry off, I felt like I had the bubble guts.

"This the wrong fucking time to shit!" I fussed as I headed to the toilet.

When my mission was complete, I slipped back into the shower to rewash myself and didn't get out until I felt completely fresh. By then, I was pressed for time. Now I had to hurry to my closet to put some threads together.

"Looking sharp there bruh," I smiled at my reflection in the dusty mirror. It was definitely time to get someone over to do some spring cleaning.

Satisfied with my appearance, I grabbed my keys, phone, and wallet before leaving my house. Now I had to go scoop my boy up.

Miguel lived half an hour from me but fifteen minutes from downtown. There was this upscale club that recently opened that I had been meaning to check out. Maybe it was time to check it out and step my game up with the ladies. I needed to fuck with a bitch that had her own dough. One who wouldn't depend on me to take care of her ass. Someone who could do for me when push came to shove.

"This shit is gonna be poppin'," Miguel said sounding all hyped up as he hopped in my ride.

"How you know?" I questioned.

"About a dozen people on my social media are going live from there right now," he explained as we headed to the club.

Thank goodness that it only took a few minutes to get there because during that short ride, all I had to listen to was this nigga hyping the club up. They should've hired his little 'Cole' from the show 'Martin' looking ass to promote for them. This dude was all in and it only got worse when we got there and went inside. While he was amped up and on ten, I walked in, prepared to play it cool for the next bitch I was about to scoop up and give this pipe to.

"Damn, this club is jumping, though," I mumbled to myself as I spotted a couple of beauties standing by the bar.

Shit, before I could say something to Miguel, some big booty light skinned chick whisked him off to the dance floor. They were both over the top with it.

As I turned away from them, I made my way to the bar and stood next to a tall, leggy chick with a silver mini skirt and a black top without sleeves. She was cute with curly brown hair and a nice body.

While I was checking her out, I waved my hand at the bartender to flag him over so I could order a drink. That must've gotten the chicks attention because next thing I knew, she was entering my personal space.

"Hey there handsome," the girl flirted as she moved closer to me.

"Wassup," I replied not wanting to show too much interest.

Any female that spoke first or made the first move was usually thirsty and broke.

Since that was what I wasn't looking for, I quickly turned back to the bartender who was now in front of me asking me what I wanted to drink. "What can I get ya?"

"Yea, gimme a double shot of Henny and a gin and juice," I ordered.

"Care to buy a girl a drink?" the chick boldly asked.

"I don't even know your name," I responded.

"Ashleigh… spelled A–s–h–l–e–i–g–h."

"Yea, I can buy you a drink." The bartender put my drinks on the bar, and I said, "Give her another one of whatever that is."

"And one for my friend, Sheila," she slipped in.

"And get her friend whatever she's drinking too," I added ready to move right on along.

That begging shit was aggravating and once I was done paying for these drinks, I was getting the fuck up away from these mooching broads. I mean, from afar they looked good as fuck, but up close, naw. They were no different than the other bitches who went out and looked for a nigga to pay for shit.

"Here you go, man," the bartender yelled out over the music.

After he gave the two females their drinks and collected the money from me, they wanted to thank me and continue to grin up in my face. When I tried to walk away, Ashleigh grabbed my arm and pushed up on me.

"I'm sorry, I didn't get your name," Ashleigh spoke slyly.

Shit, she didn't get my name because I hadn't given it. Now here she was putting me on the spot again. I hated that.

"Shawn," I replied as I downed my shot and put the glass back on the bar. "My name is Shawn."

After I chanted my name off twice because she didn't hear me the first time over the loud music, I tried to escape again, but Ashleigh stood in front of me. She actually blocked my path just so she could try to flirt some more with me.

"Save me a dance," she said with a wink.

"Yea, sure."

The way that I spun around and walked away from this Ashleigh girl, had me laughing to myself. Save her a damn dance? Hell, naw. I had no intention on saving her any damn dance. She could kiss my fucking ass with her broke self!

As I walked the floor still amused by the bold female's up in there, I searched for the right one to catch my attention. That was when I laid my eyes on someone I didn't want to see. Yep, my baby mama.

The way that Doreen was on the dance floor backing it up on some nigga, made me do a double take. Oh, she could do that shit but wanted to get mad when I did it! Oh, hell naw!

"Now why the fuck she here instead of at home with Laya anyhow?" I mumbled under my breath.

If she wanted to go out and kick it with her friends, she should've called me to watch our daughter instead of paying one of her underaged cousins to do it. What sense did any of the shit make?

"Oh, I bet she up in here with her sidekick too," I whispered to myself.

Sure enough, I spotted Frankie twerking on my brother not too far from Doreen and her square ass nigga. Now I was really heated! I could've been at home watching *The Proud Family* with my baby girl instead of in this damn club, but my baby mama called herself punishing me! This was some straight bullshit!

Had that been me on the floor with another bitch, Doreen would have wanted to check me. Yet she could act like a fucking thot, and I was expected to just watch. Make no mistake about it. I wanted to check her ass, but not for dancing with that nigga! For leaving my little girl with someone other than her daddy while she got her freak on!

Right now, I wasn't going to act the fool, but when Doreen stopped dancing, I would definitely be waiting for her. If needed be, I would have to check my brother's ass too because he could've told me that my baby mama was here. And he couldn't say that he didn't know because he was dancing right next to her.

To find someone to dance with me so that Doreen could see that I was there, I turned and checked for Ashleigh, but she wasn't by the bar anymore. "Looking for me?" she asked from behind me.

"As a matter of fact, I was," I confessed.

Ashleigh smiled as I grabbed her hand and led her to the dance floor. It didn't take long for Doreen to make her way over to where we were dancing.

"What the fuck Shawn!" she fussed.

"Go back and do yo thang with ol' boy! Why you bothering me?" I asked as I continued to dance with Ashleigh.

"I know you ain't ignoring me!" Doreen yelled.

"Go on with that shit, Doreen! I ain't trying to start no shit with you."

"You must be if you in here dancing with this... this... this THOT!!"

Ashleigh immediately stopped dancing. "Okay, now I don't know what the hell is going on between y'all..."

WHAP!

Doreen didn't waste any time lashing out the way she always did. What she wasn't expecting as she stood there smugly, was for Ashleigh to start swinging on her. As the two got to exchanging blows, Frankie rushed over to jump in, but I stopped her.

"Uh, uh! This a one on one!" I yelled.

"Get out the fucking way Shawn!" Frankie hollered as she fought to get loose from my grip.

"Aye! I said NO!"

While the two continued to duke it out, Ashleigh started to get the best of Doreen. They were now creating such an uproar that security was on their way.

As I watched the big, buffed guys break through the crowd, I pulled Ashleigh off my baby mama. That way, I could possibly keep the two of them from ending up in jail.

As I rushed Ashleigh through the door leading outside, I heard Doreen screaming from behind me. I didn't even know where Miguel was, but if he wasn't outside by the car when I reached it, I was leaving his ass.

"Let go of me, Shawn!" Ashleigh yelled as she tried to break free.

"Nah, lemme get you home! If you stay here, you just gon fight again!" I stated.

"Ain't no need for me to fight again! I won!"

"Right, but you don't know my baby mama! She's gonna come back for you..."

"Then let her!" she stated with a smug smile. "I will whoop her ass again!"

"Do you wanna go to jail Ashleigh?" I asked.

"No, but if that's what she wants, I'm cool with it. My uncle will have me out before they shut the cell doors."

What? Finally, a bitch that was tough enough that Doreen wouldn't be able to run off! Who would've thought?

Chapter Four

Doreen Collins

"Take your fucking hands of me!" I yelled as security put me out the club and held onto me long enough for Shawn to leave with the bitch that I was fighting with. "Who was that bitch, Frankie?"

"That chick has hands!" Frankie gasped with her fist up to her mouth like she was clowning me or some shit.

"Fuck you!"

"No, seriously, Doreen. That bitch was matching every punch you threw blow for blow. Had you going toe to toe with that ho'."

"Fuck all that noise you yappin' about, Frankie. Who is she?"

"Ashleigh Brown."

"And who the fuck is Ashleigh Brown?!"

"She owns a gym over on the south side. She's into all that boxing and shit..."

"Wow! So, the bitch is a boxer... like Layla Ali or some shit!" I questioned.

"Yea, bitch! That ho' can fight too! I ain't never seen her in action like that before, but..."

"What the hell does that mean?"

"It means that I've seen her fight with the gloves and shit, but this is the first time I've seen her club fighting!" she stated with a smile. "I mean, being that she's a trained fighter, it's understandable that..."

"Understandable that what? You tryna say that bitch whooped my ass, Frankie?" I asked ready to cry.

Never in all my life had I lost a fight and this one wasn't about to be my first, especially not behind Shawn's ass.

To mask my embarrassment, I had to buck up and talk shit to my best friend. I had to let her know the next time I saw that Ashleigh bitch it would be going down on sight. The next time, I would be ready for her ass, even if it meant hitting the gym twice a week.

"You better start working out and eating your Wheaties if you wanna get that bitch back. She's a tough one," Frankie warned.

"Frankie, shut the fuck up and get the hell in the car! I don't even wanna talk about that shit no more."

"Ah, I'm riding back with Square."

"What?!" I snapped. "You going over there with the enemy?"

"Well, I can't help it if my man is your baby daddy's brother. I know you don't expect me to leave my boo hanging just because you're mad right now,"

Frankie babbled. "That don't have nothing to do with me or him!"

Fuck that. I didn't want to hear a thing she had to say unless she was leaving the club with me. She had to know that I was more humiliated than I had ever been in my life. Now I had to go home and cry by myself. Ugh!

"Well, well, well, looks like the hood champ finally met her match," Square clowned as he crept up behind us.

"Shut the fuck up nigga! Why the hell didn't you tell me your brother was coming to the club? Was that a set up or some shit? Did you know he was gonna be with that bitch?" I yelled as I did everything that I could to hold back the tears.

"I'm gonna shut up. Not cuz you told me to though. Just cuz my mama always said it ain't cool to kick somebody when they down. But as much as you trying to act like that shit didn't bother you, I bet you cry when you get in yo car," Square added.

I came so close to slapping the shit out of him, but because Frankie was my best friend, I kept my hands to myself. The last thing I needed was for me and Frankie to get into it because of Square's dumb ass!

"That shit ain't funny, Square!" Frankie fussed and punched him in the arm. "That bitch Ashleigh be boxing and shit. Working out in the gym probably everyday…"

"Yea, she did a couple of moves on Doreen that I know I saw in a WWF battle," he continued to tease.

"You know what Square? You and Frankie can go head on with that bullshit! I'm about to go."

"I bet she gonna cry when she get in the car, baby," Square whispered to my best friend.

In turn, she frowned up again and pushed away from him. "You know what? Just go head on home. I'm just gonna ride back with Doreen and make sure she's cool. I'll call you later."

"Seriously, Frankie? We had plans later."

"And you done fucked that up," she stated with her hands on her hips.

"Are you for real right now?" Square asked with a confused look on his face.

"Dead ass!"

"Well damn! That don't make no sense!"

"You should've thought about that before you started running your mouth! Now, go find your brother and check that nigga for letting Ashleigh put hands on his baby mama. That shit was foul and wrong, and you know it!"

Square shrugged his shoulders and walked to his car. Once inside, he sped off out of the parking lot. Oh, well.

"You okay, girl?" Frankie asked as we climbed in my ride.

As I keyed the ignition, I began letting the tears fall. "Physically, yes. Mentally, hell no!"

"What's bothering you, D? The fact that your baby daddy was with another female or the fight y'all got into?"

"Both!" I sniffled and tried to stop crying.

"Well, I ain't tryna be funny, but how many times you done caught that nigga cheating?"

"It was different then."

"How?" Frankie pressed.

"He usually cared that I saw him with a bitch, but this time it was different. This time it seemed like he didn't care that I saw him."

"Probably because you broke up with him. In his eyes, he's single."

"I didn't break up with him. I just wanted a break."

"A break! After the way you told me you left things last time you were at his house! The way you tased that chick..."

"I didn't tase her. He did!"

"You made him!" Frankie argued. "Then you haven't been letting him see Laya! I'm sure that has a lot to do with how he feels right now."

"Whose side are you on, Frankie?" I inquired.

"Your side. Always on your side, but Doreen, how do you think Shawn felt when he saw you bumping and grinding on Jamison?"

"Jamison is just a friend."

"A friend that you used to fuck."

"Whatever, Frankie. I ain't fucking him now."

"But you have in the past and that marks him as a threat. You already knew that though and you're damn lucky Shawn don't know about him."

"Maybe he should. Hell, I know about Syanna," I argued as made it home and went inside.

"We aren't even gonna get into that shit. Let's just fix a drink and start plotting."

"Plotting for what?"

"For how you're gonna get back at that bitch Ashleigh for embarrassing us all like that."

"Shut the hell up, Frankie. Did you even try to help me? Did you at least kick or pinch the bitch?"

"Now, you know I would've if I could've, Doreen! Yo baby daddy held onto me so tight that I got bruises on my arms. Look!"

Frankie wasn't lying because I saw the marks with my own eyes. That right there was some messed up shit. My own baby daddy really let that girl get me like that.

The more I replayed the fight, the more upset I became with Shawn until I reached a decision to act on it. "I'm about to go over there."

"No, you're not!" Frankie warned. "We ain't got no back up and please don't tell me about that fucking gun. It ain't gonna do a bit of good if you get taken down first."

"You seriously being a punk right now!" I pressed. "I'm not gonna be able to sleep until I beat that bitch up..."

"And get your title back, huh Champ?" Frankie teased but quickly dropped the grin when I scowled at her. "Too soon?"

"Bitch, you lucky you're my best friend and I love you because I swear..." I sighed and said goodnight.

Between the fight and drinks, I was exhausted, and could feel a headache coming on. To alleviate the pain, I went into my bathroom and popped a couple of extra strength acetaminophen then went to shower and change. When I got out, I grabbed my phone to call Shawn.

"What do you want?"

"Why... you with that bitch?"

"That ain't yo business no more D. If it ain't about Laya, don't call me and ask me shit!"

"How you know it ain't about our daughter?" I shot back without thinking that shit through. There was nothing wrong with my daughter and I wasn't about to say that there was and jinx my baby girl.

"What's up, Doreen?" Before I had a chance to respond, he asked another question. "Why the hell you didn't call me to watch Laya if you wanted to go out tonight?"

"Laya is over at my mom's house. My little cousins Lisa and Tracey are watching her."

"Oh, so you can give them a lil change to watch my shorty, but you can't let me come get her and keep her for free? You know she misses her daddy."

As badly as I wanted to admit that I missed him too, my pride wouldn't allow it. My heart was in pain and all I wanted was to make things right. Only I couldn't do that without getting some type of payback. First person on my list was Shawn. After that, I was coming for Ashleigh.

That would give me the opportunity to at least work out for a few weeks before stepping to her again without a weapon of some sort. Not necessarily a gun, but maybe a taser. That shit really worked. I just hated to find out the hard way.

"Aight D, well, if you don't want shit, I'm about to get off here."

"You are with that bitch, huh?" I asked again.

"Why are you even worried about it. We ain't together and please don't remind me that we have a child together because you ain't let me see Laya in over a month. That's fucked up, but it's okay, you'll need me."

Shit, I needed Shawn right then, but I still couldn't humble myself and tell him that. Why?

Probably because I was brought up in a hostile environment. In our house, fighting was always the way to solve a problem. I wasn't so sure about that now.

Lately, I had been thinking that maybe I needed to find another way to resolve my issues. One that wasn't so violent.

"Doreen!" Shawn called out. "I'm about to go. I'm on the block and I got some shit to handle."

"How long we gonna be out here?" I heard a female ask in the background.

My heart pounded heavily as I asked Shawn again if Ashleigh was with him. I prayed he didn't give me the wrong answer.

"Is that her with you, Shawn?"

"Look Doreen, not that it's any of your business, but no, that's not Ashleigh. It's Rachel. I'm out here training her for Q..."

"Rachel Gwinn?!" I gasped.

"Why? What difference does it make. I'on even know why I mentioned her name. Yo' ass is trippin'. This is straight business and if you get up in this shit, you won't only have to deal with me, but you'll have to deal with Q too. Enough said?"

"Enough said," I repeated, but I didn't like it. Truthfully, I didn't like no bitch up close and personal with Shawn.

Whether our relationship was on a break or not, he was mine. All mine...

Chapter Five

Rachel Gwinn

What was I thinking when I agreed to Quinton's proposition? How the hell did I go from fucking him to working for him? And under Shawn at that.

When I went to meet him at 3am that first morning, he looked just as annoyed as I felt. Unlike me, he spoke up about it.

"Look Rachel, I know you're familiar with these streets and all, but out here, you gotta be careful."

"So, Shawn, I'm gonna be slanging on the block?" I gasped.

Yea, I was tough, but not crazy. There was no way I was doing that shit.

"No, I'm gonna have you straight collecting," he explained. "The only time you have to get out is when you go to the trap houses."

"Where the crackheads be at?"

"Hell naw! Our spots deal strictly with prescription drugs. They are all nice properties, so you won't be dealing with the street bullshit unless you gotta pick up from the hustlers on the block and Benji usually does that."

"Oh, so I need to dress up a little, huh?" I clowned as I got a little excited.

"It would be nice. I don't need you walking up into a million dollar estate looking like you straight hood. Play the part."

"Gotcha." I smiled and watched Shawn check his phone. It was the third time his baby mama called him.

Since I knew Doreen didn't have the good sense that the Lord gave her, I didn't ask a single question. I was going to stay out of that one.

"That chick is crazy."

"You need to get that again?" I asked as I checked my cell for the time.

"Naw, let's go."

That morning, Shawn must've taken me to ten different spots to pick up. I had to learn the routes, the days and the contact's name. It was a lot but after I met Senior Rico, out in the hills, my job became much more exciting.

"Aight, that's it for today, but I'm gonna warn you right now. You need to chill," Shawn stated as we pulled up to where I left my car.

"Chill? What you mean?"

"Yo, I peeped you checking out Rico. You think Doreen is loco! Well, she ain't got shit on Rico's wife, Dominque. That bitch is a stone- cold killer."

"That nigga fine, but this is all business. It don't hurt to look though."

"It might be deadly to look in this game we're in. Don't say that I didn't warn you, Rachel."

"Bye, Shawn," I replied and hopped out of his ride.

Whatever Shawn was talking about didn't scare me in the least. If I saw something I liked, I went after it. Not saying that I was interested in Senor Rico like that. Just saying that the dude was fine. And Shawn was right about one thing, I couldn't keep my eyes off his sexy body.

No matter how many guys I came across and found attractive, none of them could compare to Quinton. He was not only handsome; he was very smart. That was how he got into the position he was in... a boss position.

"Let me call him right now and tell him all about my day." I giggled as I kicked off my shoes and plopped down on my bed.

That laughing ceased as soon as I found out that I was still blocked. What the hell?

All this shit that I was willing to do just to stay close to Quinton was continuously backfiring on me. That gave me the idea to maybe use a different approach. Like focusing on Justice instead of her husband. That way I could find out exactly what was going on behind closed doors. I had plenty of questions to ask. Things that I needed to know.

Starting with... were Quinton and Justice really in love, or was it a marriage used for the purpose of keeping her out of the system? Whichever it was, I should've been told too. I mean, I was involved in this equation whether Quinton wanted to admit it or not.

I still couldn't believe he had married my best friend. Of all the chicks he could have married, why would he choose the one that meant the most to me? Knowing that Justice had lost her mom, I was looking to step in and be there for her. But Quinton had gotten to her before I did.

How did he get to Justice so fast anyway? I mean, her mom was killed, and she had just left my place. I had been searching for her the whole time and she had been with Quinton. How did he know that she would need someone? Why when he found her, he didn't bring her to my mom's house?

He knew what she meant to me. how close we were. He should have known that she would need me. Instead, he ran away with her. Then showed up married to her.

The way that they even ended up together was puzzling and aggravating at the same time. For whatever the reason, I wasn't just going to accept that shit and let him get away with how he treated me. I had to think of something...

The situation baffled me all night and I woke up the next morning with only one thing on my mind... getting in touch with Quinton. If he couldn't give me the answers that I needed, then he could at least give me some good dick.

So what if he was married to Justice now. I was almost certain that he wasn't fucking her. If he was, he would've admitted that shit when I asked him. Instead, he froze up and changed the subject.

Quinton should've known that I was aware of my best friend's 'virgin' status, and he wasn't going to be the one to take it away from her. Ring on her finger or not, Justice wasn't just going to give her cookies up if the man wasn't special to her.

If he was, she definitely didn't seem like she was in love when she came to my place. She seemed sad and a bit distant. Naw, they weren't in love, and they certainly weren't fucking. That meant Quinton would be in need of some good sex soon.

That was where I would come in and do all three of us a favor by giving Quinton some of my cookies. That way, he wouldn't have to risk getting any sexually transmitted diseases by fucking someone out of our circle. One thing about me, I got tested at least twice a year to make sure that I was good in that department.

If only I could come up with another way to get Quinton's attention without Justice finding out. I loved my best friend, but if I had to be sneaky and hide my affair with her husband, I was distressed enough to do just that.

"Maybe I can make another social media account or get a second cell..." I thought aloud.

Since Quinton had my phone and all of my online accounts blocked, those were the only ways that I could get in touch with him. Desperate times called for desperate measures and since he made me fall for him so hard, I hoped that he didn't think that it was going to be that easy to rid of me.

What did he expect me to do without him? Just move on like what we had never existed.

Quinton couldn't have possibly thought that. He couldn't have possibly thought that marrying Justice would make me back off.

That wasn't even an option. Not when I was addicted to the way he loved me.

Quinton had the best dick I ever had. Ever since the first time we had sex, I had been dickmatized. There I said it... I was dickmatized.

When a man gave you some good dick like Quinton gave me, it was hard not to become attached to it. I didn't intend to fall this hard for Q because I already had a man when we started fucking around.

As I laid across my bed, I thought about how things started between me and Quinton...

The first night we really kicked it was when he took me out to dinner for my eighteenth birthday. That was also the same night I proved my loyalty by killing a dude for him.

In turn, Quinton took me to a very nice hotel and got us some massages and drinks. It wasn't like I had planned to sleep with him, but we just started kissing and touching on each other, and the next thing I knew, he had his dick in my mouth. Well, once the dick slid down my throat, things quickly picked up from there.

All I remembered was screaming Quinton's name until two o'clock the next morning. He must have slipped out of our hotel suite during the wee hours because when I woke up at eight for work, he was gone. So was I...

One dose of the dick and I was as addicted to his dick as Snoop Dogg was to weed. Hell, I even thought I was in love. At least that was what I called and told him.

"You love me? Rachel, stop. I already told you that what happened between us was between us! Now you cool and I dig you and all, but that's it. I ain't for settling down and if you run yo mouth about it, it's a wrap!" he spat.

"I'm not going to tell anyone we had sex!" I argued. "I mean, the only way anyone can find out is if we talk right? No one knows about us but us!"

It had been that way ever since last year, but I didn't know how much longer I could hold our secret. This nigga had my heart and I wanted to shout it to the world, but I couldn't because not only was Quinton married to Justice now, but he had made it clear that he didn't want anything to do with me. That shit hurt my feelings.

"Fuck it! Sometimes you gotta outsmart a muthafucka to make him listen," I chanted lowly once I finished making a new social media page.

Now it was time to send Quinton a message. Hopefully, he would care enough to respond...

Me: I know you didn't think I was smart enough to make another page but guess what! I am! Now, I miss you and I'm tired of you ignoring me, so I need to see you. If you don't come by my place today, whether it be before or after 5, IDGAF!! Just make sure you bring your ass over here or I'm gonna tell Justice all about our lil arrangement starting with how long we been having sex. Idk about your thoughts but I think my bestie would be real interested in hearing that we been fucking since last year!

The second that I sent that message, my heart sank to my stomach. It was the anxiety caused by the uncertainty of how Quinton would react.

Hopefully, he wouldn't mistake it as a threat because everyone, including me, was well aware that he didn't take threats lightly. If he did, I would have to get prepared for whatever.

At this point, I didn't care how he felt. I was tired playing these games with Quinton.

KNOCK! KNOCK! KNOCK!

My chest jumped as my thoughts disbursed and I rushed towards the door. There was no way that Quinton came to my apartment instead of messaging me back. He had to be angry.

In fear that it was actually him, I quietly got up on my tiptoes and looked through the peephole. Shit! It was Quinton.

While I had been waiting for him to message me back, two and a half hours later, I guess he decided to drive over instead. His unannounced visit had me confused and I didn't know whether to be happy to finally see him or scared for my life because I had been playing beyond the boundaries.

"Open the door, Rachel!" Quinton yelled as he continued to bang. "I know you're in there! You wanted to see me, huh? Well, I'm here, so open the damn door!"

As desperately as I wanted to ignore him, I knew that I couldn't hide forever. Not when he ran the same streets that I had to run through every day.

"I'm coming dang!" I whined as I finally got up enough nerve to swing the door open. Soon as I did, I regretted it.

"What the fuck you send that message for?" he asked with rage written all over his face. "Were you threatening me Rachel?"

"No, no! I wasn't trying to threaten you!" I denied.

"The fuck you weren't! You said if you didn't hear from me, you were gonna tell Justice about us! That sure sounds like a fuckin' threat to me!"

"I didn't mean it to be!" I whined. "I just wanted to see and talk to you! It's been so long..."

"I don't give a fuck! Don't be making random threats to me muthafucka! Whether you like it or not, I'm married to Justice now!"

"Why did you do that though?" I cried, unable to hold back the tears any longer. "Why did you marry her knowing she's my best friend? Were you trying to hurt me?"

"Girl please! Are you fa real right now?"

"Yes, I'm fa real!"

"You can't be! Either you're in denial or just fucking deaf, Rachel. Why the hell do I have to keep repeating myself?"

"Because I don't fucking understand, Q. I don't understand how this could have happened! Please make it make sense! You had to have married her to shut her up about something or to get back at me!" I blurted out.

"I can promise you like I did before, that when I said 'I do' to Justice, you were the furthest thing from my mind. I married Justice cuz I wanted to..."

"Are you fucking her?" I inquired.

"Didn't we just have this conversation already, Rachel? Why you keep asking me the same shit yo?"

"Yea, but you didn't answer me then and you seem to be sidestepping the question now. Which is it?"

"I don't answer to you!"

"Just be honest! Are you fucking my best friend?"

"That ain't yo business!"

"I just can't understand why you would ruin what we have for Justice. What the hell makes her more special than me?" I asked, not sure if I even wanted to know the answer.

"She's my wife!"

"But why? You don't love her, and you damn sho' ain't sleeping with her!"

"How the hell would you know that?" he asked.

"You had such a problem having sex with me until I became of age, so I know you aren't screwing her! And if you're not getting it from her, you might as well get it from me," I suggested as I reached for him.

Quinton held his hand out to stop me then backed away. "Whoa nah! We ain't about to have sex," he clarified.

"What?" I asked feeling my emotions deflate.

"Did I stutter?" he joked.

"Why not? I'm sure Justice wouldn't mind me taking one for the team to help her out..."

Apparently, Quinton found humor in what I said because he threw his head back and laughed loudly. Then he narrowed his eyes at me and asked, "Help her out? How the hell would you be helping her out by sleeping with me?"

"Because as much as you like to fuck, if she's not giving it to you, I'd rather you get it from me than someone else. It's called helping out my friend," I explained as I reached for him again.

Just as Quinton had done before, he backed away from me and made it clear that he wanted nothing to do with me physically. "Nah. It ain't going down," he echoed.

The seriousness in his eyes along with his voice warned me to do as he said and step back. But damn. Why was he refusing me?

Chapter Six

Quinton Marshall

The nerve of Rachel's fucking ass! That bitch made a whole new page just to get at me. Then she had the audacity to threaten me! The only reason I came over to her place was to remind her once again that we were absolutely done!

How many times was I going to have to repeat myself without taking action? This chick was still overstepping her boundaries.

What was it going to take for Rachel to listen? What was it going to take to make her believe that nothing was going to change the way that I felt?

"We are done Rachel! I can't tell you that enough times. What other way do I have to say this shit to make you understand?"

"I don't believe you! If we were really done, you wouldn't be here right now!"

"We are definitely done! The only reason I'm here is to tell you to your damn face! And if you even think about talking to Justice about us, you will be sorry. And knowing me the way that you do, you know that I don't make idle threats."

"Wow! Seriously! You're really done..."

"Fuckin' right! I took the vows I said to Justice very seriously."

"That's crazy. You don't even care that I still love you!" she inquired.

Why the fuck should I care if she still loved me or not? The only person I was worried about was Justice and her feelings for me. I was concerned about whether our marriage would be successful and what could be done to improve how things were going.

"Nope. All I care about is my wife and making sure that she knows that I am there for her," I said. "I can't be there for her if I'm screwing your ass. So, as long as I have a wife at home, know that I won't EVER need to fuck you or any other chick for that matter."

"It's not even a real marriage!" she argued.

"It's as real as this apartment that we're standing in," I countered. "Now that this conversation is over, I'm gonna head home to my WIFE! What you need to do is get with Shawn so he can put your ass to work!"

When I finished what I was saying, I turned to leave and shook my head. I was so fucking done with Rachel's crazy ass!

"So, that's it!" she continued to whine.

"Yep. That's it! Get you a life Rachel! Find you another man to give your pussy to and focus on getting your paper. Shawn said you made a little grip last shift!" I stated.

"That's all I am to you now... one of your fucking workers?" Rachel cried as she chased me to the door.

"Yes, I see now you get it," I clowned as I walked right on out of there.

Rachel called after me, but I paid her no attention. She had gotten on my nerves for the last time. I mean, a bitch could only aggravate you as long as you allowed her to. It was time to cut her ass off...

Surprisingly, I found it easier than I thought to stay away from Rachel for the next few weeks. But now that Justice was turning eighteen, I wasn't so sure if I could keep her at bay...

Three weeks later...

Today was Justice's eighteenth birthday, a day I had been waiting on for the longest time. I climbed out of bed early this morning to plan something special for her. To start it all off, I called over to her favorite restaurant and ordered everything she liked.

It must've been around 9am when they delivered the food. Right on time.

After I pulled everything out the bags and got it all situated on the serving tray, I grabbed a bottle of chilled champagne to go with the orange juice that I had already poured into a carafe. With the celebratory bottle and food in hand, I went and woke Justice up so that I could serve her in bed. As she rubbed her eyes in an effort to focus on her surroundings, I watched how her facial expressions shifted.

"What is all this?" Justice asked as her eyes filled with tears.

Before I answered her question, I placed the tray over her lap and poured us both a mimosa. Once I handed her a glass, I joined her to stare at the candles, red mylar heart shaped balloons and the six dozen bouquets of red roses that I had already set out.

"I just wanted today to be special for you. Happy birthday, babe!" I cheered as I leaned over and kissed her forehead.

"I can't believe you did all this for me!" Justice stated as she grabbed a Kleenex from the nightstand and dabbed at her tears.

"I'm glad you like the surprise."

"I do! Thank you so much," she said happily.

As I stood there and witnessed the joy in her face, I couldn't help but smile. Oh, but I wasn't done yet.

"I have one more surprise for you this morning," I confessed as I walked over to the dresser where I had a special gift waiting for her.

As soon as she saw the bag, her mouth dropped. "No, you did not buy me something from Tiffany's!" she shrieked.

"I did."

"WHAT!! Are you kidding me?!" she continued.

"No, I wanted something special to make this birthday memorable for you," I explained.

"It's already memorable because today I'm finally eighteen, which means I don't have to hide from anyone anymore!" she triumphed. "Besides, you didn't have to spend that much money on me. You already bought me this big ass ring!" She held her hand up.

"Money is no object when it comes to you, babe."

"That's good to know. Can I see it?"

"I thought you didn't want it," I teased.

"Stop it!" Justice joked as she laughed and reached for the bag.

As I handed it to her, she quickly pulled out the turquoise- colored box with the white ribbon on top. She opened the box and started screaming.

"Oh MY GOD!! It's beautiful!"

It was a diamond bracelet with huge circular shaped diamonds all around and the clasp had four marquis diamonds which formed the outline of a butterfly.

"Is this white gold?" Justice asked.

"It is! You like it?"

"I love it! Will you put it on me?"

While Justice held her wrist out, I put the bracelet on. It looked exactly the way I thought it would on her.

"It's so pretty. It makes me feel glamorous," she admitted shamelessly.

"I knew it would look nice on you," I confessed as I admired how beautiful the gift looked on her wrist.

"Quinton, I can't believe you did all this for me. Did you buy breakfast for you too?"

"Yea, I just wanted to bring you yours first. Lemme go get mine," I said.

After I went to the kitchen and grabbed my food from the restaurant, I returned to the bedroom to join Justice. As we sat on the bed and commenced to eating breakfast and sipping champagne with orange juice together, we talked about what she would like to do for her special day.

"Well, you know I wanna go see Rachel. She's been so busy working some new job that I've barely gotten a chance to talk to her," Justice started. "Since I have my license, I was thinking that I could go and get her and maybe go to eat later or something."

"Go ahead and call her to see if she can hang out. We can do what I had planned this evening," I told her.

The only reason I urged Justice to call Rachel was I knew she couldn't go. Not when she was in San Antonio making some extra dough with Shawn.

Yep, I had it all planned and killed two birds with one stone while I was at it. Got Shawn away from his crazy baby mama for a minute and got Rachel out of mine. A win- win situation in my book.

"Awwwww, I didn't know you were out of town," I listened to Justice whine. "I guess we'll hook up when you get back in a few days."

"What's wrong?" I asked playing dumb as she hung up with Rachel and explained how she was in San Antonio on business for the next week.

"She must have a damn good job for them to send her out of town like that." Justice beamed like she was truly impressed, but then instantly started to pout. "But that's a whole week away before I get to hang out with her."

"It's okay, baby. I have something planned this weekend anyhow."

"I'm more than grateful for what you've already done, Quinton. You don't have to do nothing else?"

"Not even take you on a lil honeymoon. You know... since we didn't have one."

"Say what?"

"I mean, that's if you wanna go to the Virgin Islands."

"What?" Justice gasped then frowned. "Wait, don't I need a passport to go there?"

"No, we're going to St. Thomas. It's part of the U.S."

"Are you serious, Q? You're really taking me to some tropical island getaway?"

"If you wanna go, I have the flight, rental, and resort already booked and paid for," I revealed as I poured the last of the champagne in Justice's glass.

"Shit, say less. I'm gonna pack tonight."

"Pack light..." I sang out trying to be funny.

I knew I was pushing it by taking Justice away from here, but I couldn't risk her chilling and getting comfy with Rachel before I had a chance to tell her about us. Knowing Rachel the way that I did, if she did beat me to the punch, she would find a way to twist that shit and make Justice hate me. I had to find a way to tell Justice before Rachel got the chance. The trip would be the perfect time. Only if I could find the words by them.

Shit, how was I supposed to tell Justice something like that without ruining everything? I didn't know what the fuck to say. I mean, how the fuck did I tell her that I had been fucking her friend before we got married?

No nigga wanted to admit no shit like that! Especially me.

With the trust issues that Justice already had concerning me made it difficult to reveal my secrets. What really had me hesitant were the side eyes and smart remarks she gave me whenever we discussed her mother or anything that reminded her of her.

Even though we were married, I knew that in the back of her mind, she still wondered if I had something to do with her mom's death. Shit, I did, but I didn't want her to know that! If I could spare her the pain of finding that out, I was ready to take that secret to my grave.

The longer I kept her from finding out, the more I could work on getting her to trust me. And once I got her to fully trust me, she would forget all about her intuitions about my involvement in her mom getting killed. If she didn't, we would deal with that if and when that time came.

"You are so corny sometimes," Justice cracked with a giggle causing my worries to momentarily fade.

As I glanced over at her, I couldn't stop marveling at her natural beauty. No other chick I had ever fucked with could touch her.

"Why are you staring at me like that, Q?" she asked with a bashful grin. "You must be feeling this champagne like I am."

"Yea, that shit got a punch, but that's not what got me trippin'."

"What is it then?"

"I can't believe you're finally eighteen, baby," I blurted out.

The day that I had been waiting for since I married Justice. Now, maybe... just maybe, I could get close enough to get her to consummate it.

"I can't believe I'm eighteen either, but then again, let me keep it real, Q. I've been feeling grown ever since you gave me that fake ID," she confessed boldly as she tilted her glass and finished her drink.

"I knew it, baby. I knew it. And you better hold onto that shit too. You got three more years to go to be legally 21," I reminded.

"Oh, I am."

As we sat in our bedroom, I opened another bottle of champagne while Justice went on and on about our upcoming trip. What she was saying sounded more like distant chatter to my ears because all I could concentrate on was actually getting across the line with her. No more keeping it casual by cuddling all night until we fell asleep. Now it was time for some lovemaking, and I couldn't fucking wait.

"Well, what are we gonna do today?" she questioned as she gathered our mess from breakfast and stacked it neatly on the tray.

When I saw her stumbling a bit, I rushed over to help her. "Whatever you wanna do."

As we went down to the kitchen to throw away the trash, I noticed how tipsy Justice really was. "I wanna hear some music."

From the table to the counter, she flew over to the Echo Show so that she could turn on some old school tunes. The first songs that played had Justice doing all the dances from the past. She was shaking that ass so hard that she had my dick standing up.

"Come on, Q!" she begged. "Come dance with me."

Soon as Justice took hold of my hands, a slow song came on. Now, that was more my speed. With my body on hers, I knew she had to feel my monster rising again. She confirmed it when the music shifted, and her hand went directly to my dick.

"Shit!" I moaned.

It was the first time in a minute that someone's hand was on my shaft other than my own. The shit felt so good that I almost busted prematurely. Something that I hadn't done since I was a teenager.

"Somebody is excited," Justice acknowledged and giggled as she continued to massage my hardness until the precum soiled the front of my shorts.

"Let's go upstairs and shower," I suggested with one thing on my mind. Some bomb ass foreplay that included oral sex. Both of us needed to be nice and fresh for that shit.

To lead her up to the master bedroom, I grabbed ahold of my wife's hand and flirted with her all the way up the stairs. She had me so worked up by the time we made it there, I was almost ready to say fuck that shower until Justice started to undress in front of me for the first time.

"Shit!" I gasped in a whisper as I was finally able to see her in raw form from head to toe.

"You gonna join me in the shower?" she slurred with a giggle.

"Are you serious?" I checked before I eagerly exposed myself in record time. I certainly didn't want to look like a fool if we weren't on the same page.

"Do I look serious?"

Justice waltzed into the opening that led to the master bathroom and started the water. As she held her hand under the forceful streams, she turned her head towards me and hungrily eyed me down.

With that clear clue, I swiftly stripped down to nothing and escorted her into the clear octagon shaped enclosure. "Oh, my!" Justice gasped as I found her focus glued to my dick that was proudly standing up at attention. It was like that muthafucka was saluting the pussy before attacking it.

"Stop trippin'!" I laughed as a bashful feeling swept across me.

Justice was so innocent, and I was beginning to rethink this aggressive approach that was pressing me to just dive into it. With her, I needed to take things slow. Maybe start with some of that foreplay that I was thinking about earlier.

I wonder if she would be down for that shit...

Chapter Seven

Justice Patterson

"Oh, shit, yes!" I moaned as Quinton licked me up and down like a lollipop while the relaxing bursts of water hit my backside.

As his tongue swirled around my left nipple, his hands gently gripped my ass. The pleasure was so great that the sensation between my thighs quickly increased.

"Fuck, yes!" I yelled as the pressure continued to build.

All the stuff I heard and seen on TV about sex couldn't have prepared me for the incredible experience that Quinton was introducing me to. It had every inch of my body tingling, and I didn't want it to stop.

"Whoa!" I gasped when he lifted my left thigh and rested it on his wide muscular shoulder.

Without warning, he went down face first.

"Oh, fuck! What are you doing to me?" I gasped as he took his tongue game to my clit and stimulated it until I yelled out his name.

"Quinton!"

As I used one hand to hold on to the top of the shower door, I used the other to grip the back of Quinton's head. Next thing I knew, I was humping his face. I didn't stop until I reached my climax.

"Shit! This is what it feels like?" I panted as I began to feel dizzy.

While my head spun and my tummy bubbled, my pussy was still throbbing and craving more. As much as I wanted to go to the toilet and vomit, the hunger I had for sex was stronger.

To attempt to shake it off, I opened my mouth and let some water in so that I could swallow a couple of times. That definitely didn't help.

"Ugh!" I grunted then chucked up the food from breakfast right along with all the champagne we ingested.

"Fuck! Are you okay, baby?" he panicked as he rinsed off the gross particles that managed to splash on him.

"Talk about embarrassing!" I whispered as I went to the sink to rinse my mouth and brush my teeth.

"Shit, don't be embarrassed."

"I just threw up all over you during our very first real intimate moment together, Q! That shit is nasty and hella embarrassing!" I reminded as I spit in the sink and realized that I was still butt ass naked with water dripping everywhere.

After I retrieved a towel off the wall mounted rack, I wrapped it around me then looked up at Quinton. His sincere smile comforted me and so did his strong arms when he embraced me.

"We have plenty of time to share those moments. Don't even trip."

"Yea, but still. It was about to be our first time and as nervous as I was, believe me, I was looking forward to it."

"Well, you did cum, didn't you?" he asked like he was the one who was ashamed.

"That's what made me so dizzy," I confessed and laughed at myself. "Shit, the feeling was so fucking good it made my body convulse. At least that's what it felt like."

We both stood there laughing and what was even more humorous, Quinton's large member was on the rise again. Even after I vomited all over him!

While he obviously had coochie on the brain, I wasn't the least bit interested at the moment. Right now, all I wanted to do was lay down for an hour or two. After that, maybe we could discuss it.

"Wake up sleepy head!" Quinton hollered out as he gently shook me until my eyes opened. "I'm not about to let you sleep your birthday away. Come on."

"What? Where are we going?" I asked as I sat up and noticed that he was fully dressed in a blue Nike sweatsuit with matching sneakers.

From what I saw him wearing, sex was no longer on his mind. What he was talking about now was going out to eat.

"We got reservations at this dope ass spot," Quinton explained. "Oh, and don't forget your ID."

"Why? I'm definitely not drinking for a couple of days. I need to fully recuperate for our trip to the Virgin Islands."

Shit, the way things were going, I was still going to be a virgin when I got over there. What the fuck?

"You'll need it to sit in the private bar area. You don't have to drink, baby. I just wanna get you outside for some fresh air and get you something good to eat."

"I am starving."

Since I had emptied my stomach of all of its contents it was starting to growl now. That ginger ale and those crackers that Quinton had left next to the bed weren't nearly enough to satisfy my appetite.

"Give me twenty minutes and I'll be down," I told him as I climbed out of the bed and went to shower.

When I noticed that there was no trace of the mess I had made earlier, I thanked Quinton and apologized again. "No worries, baby. That's what I'm here for... to take care of my wife."

After a quick kiss and a pat on my ass, he disappeared and gave me the privacy I desired. To use it wisely, I hurried to grab a nice outfit. A hot pink Puma hoodie with the joggers and white leather sneakers to go with it.

Once out of the shower and dressed, I felt like a brand- new woman. Thank goodness too because I had a pretty good notion that Quinton was going to have me out all day and night. He was ready to celebrate like it was his damn birthday.

"You ready?" he asked as he stepped into the bedroom and checked me out. "Never mind. I see that you are and looking damn good at that."

"Thanks. Flattery will get you everywhere," I lied because Quinton's words would get him nowhere. Not unless he was confessing his sins. Then and only then would they be important enough to listen to.

Now our intimate link was something different. It was like a silent connection and for that right there, we didn't need any words. All we needed was some great sex that would leave us both satisfied.

Other than that, I was about to ride this shit out and get everything that I could from it before things came crashing to an end. Or at least, that was how I planned it...

"Where are we going?" I asked while I tried to focus on the matter at hand. Food.

"You'll see," Quinton answered as he whisked me down the stairs and out the front door where a driver was waiting.

"We're not taking your car?"

"No, we're taking yours."

"This Lincoln?"

"Yes, I just hired this dude to drive us around so that I could sit in the back and concentrate on you, birthday girl."

When Quinton handed me the main set of keys to the black MKX, I couldn't believe it. "Thank you so much, but if you do one more extravagant thing for me today, I'm gonna lose my fucking mind, Q."

"Well then, be prepared to lose that beautiful mind of yours because the day is far from over." He smiled as he helped me into the back seat before climbing in himself. Such a gentleman when he wanted to be.

The way he was catering to me made me feel like a queen and I was about to enjoy every minute of it. Starting with the fancy restaurant that he took me to on some lake. There, he not only hand fed me fruit before dinner, but he let me order whatever I wanted. Even when he knew that I wasn't going to eat it.

While we enjoyed our delicious meal, Quinton added to my list of surprises when he had some soulful singers perform a love song for me. It was so touching. Now, the only treat left was me getting some sex.

When we left there, I just knew we were about to go to the house and finish what we started earlier. To make sure Quinton would be ready, I reached over and massaged his dick through his nice jeans just as we jumped on the highway.

As it rose nicely like I anticipated, his cell began to sound off. Once, twice then a third time. That was when he answered it.

"What's up granny?"

"Where are you, Q?" I heard her yell from the passenger seat.

"Right outside the city. Why?" I inquired.

"How quick can you get here?"

"Maybe twenty minutes or so. Why, what's wrong? Are you okay?"

The worried expression that Quinton now wore let me know that something was going on with his grandmother. Although I hadn't met her yet, I wanted to help if possible.

Since my mother was no longer around, and I really missed her, I often found myself longing for her motherly love. Maybe that was what was making me so concerned about Quinton's grandmother. It had to be that maternal attachment which was now absent in my life.

"You called the cops, granny? For what? What happened?"

"I killed him! I killed Robert."

"Robert? Who the heck is Robert and what the hell happened granny?"

"I'll explain when you get here, Quinton. Just come now!"

"I'm on my way."

"What's wrong?" I questioned as he set his cell on his lap.

"I don't know, shit. She over there talking about she killed somebody!"

"What? Do you think she really did?" I gasped.

"I don't know, but whatever is going on, I know it has to be something serious to have my grandmother freaking out like that!" he told me as he gave the driver his grandmother's address.

Fifteen minutes later, we were entering a beautiful, gated community. I couldn't even take in the scenery because as soon as we rounded the corner, we saw nothing but a bunch of emergency vehicles with flashing lights. There were police and first responders everywhere.

As the ambulance drove off without the lights flashing, my stomach dropped. The whole scene caused flashbacks of the day my mother got killed.

If it wasn't for Quinton's grandmother running out in her housecoat, with her wig tilted a little too much on the left side, looking a hot mess, I would've gone into a dark place. Thanks to the sight of her, I was busting out in tears laughing instead.

"What's so funny?" Quinton asked with a cackle as he instructed the driver where to pull over. "I know you not laughing at my granny?"

"I'm so sorry, Q."

"Nah, I'm just joking. Let's get out and see what's going on. She ain't in handcuffs, so it must not be too bad."

Soon as our driver parked my car, Quinton's grandmother rushed to his side and yanked open the door, but he didn't get out. "Quinton, I killed him!"

"Ma'am, calm down," the female officer urged as she walked up to the car. "This wasn't your fault. I mean, there was nothing you could have done to prevent what happened. The guy had a heart attack."

"Yea, while I was riding on top of him! I would have never rocked his world like that if I had known he had a bad heart! Why didn't he tell me?"

"I have no idea ma'am, but that was definitely something he should have told you about," the officer said as she shook her head.

Some of the cars pulled off, as well as the ambulance and fire truck. As hard as I tried to suppress the laughter, it was nearly impossible. The shit was funny and then again, it wasn't because Quinton's grandmother was right. That man should've told her about his bad heart.

But that was just how men were. Withholding pertinent health information so they wouldn't risk the chance of not being able to hit it. Men were selfish like that. If it wasn't money over everything for them, it was without a doubt pussy over everything. Damn shame...

"Quinton, I'm going to jail!" his grandmother expressed. She was so upset that I kind of felt bad for laughing a few moments ago.

"Ma'am, I can assure you that you are not going to jail," the officer repeated as she tried to calm his grandmother down. "How about you go in the house and try to relax? Then when you're ready, you can make arrangements to..."

"Whoa! Robert wasn't my man! He belonged to Betty down the street, but she just left him. He just came over here looking for comfort, so like a good neighbor, I tried to make him feel better. I wasn't planning to have sex with him, but the shit just happened. I sure wasn't trying to cause his death!"

"I guess she still got it!" one of the neighbors shouted out causing the nearby crowd to erupt in laughter.

"You damn right I do! Now mind your damn business, Belinda!" Quinton's grandmother hollered out with her wig still barely hanging on. She blew an exasperated breath sending her lil waves of hair flying over her eyelids.

"Granny, seriously? You called me out here for this?" Quinton gasped then told her that was why he wasn't getting out of the car.

"I killed a man! Don't you think that's serious enough to call you over here?"

"But it was an accident that I would like to forget about just as quick as I found out about it. I wish I never heard about what happened, granny! Like fa real cuz all you did was paint a visual for me that I'm like... UGH!"

"Boy what? So, you don't think I got my needs just like you young folks do?" she fussed making me laugh even harder. "I guess y'all think just young people got a right to get their groove on! Well, guess what grandson! Granny got needs just like you!"

The expression on her face along with the jacked up wig and housecoat almost had me dying laughing where I stood. I didn't want her to feel like I was making fun of her or disrespecting her in any way though, so I quickly got that shit in check before she did it for me.

I must've been too loud because suddenly she looked over at me.

"Quinton, who this lil girl laughing and all up in my business?" she asked with an attitude.

"Sorry granny, this is my wife, Justice."

"Your wife! When the hell did you get a wife?" she balked.

"We been married a couple of months now," he confessed.

"The hell you mean y'all been married a couple of months?! How the hell you get married two months ago and never told me... or anybody else in the family!" His grandmother smiled and walked closer to the truck. "You're a pretty lil thing."

"Thank you, ma'am," I said as I returned the smile.

"Baby, get out this car and let me take a look at the woman who finally bagged my only grandson." She grinned as she ran around to my side and opened my door too.

Before I could get out, she was pulling me by the arm until she got me in an embrace. It was so warm that it made me feel welcomed right away.

"Oh, my goodness! Ain't you a young beauty. Quinton this is why you've been missing in action the past few months? Making me catch those Uber things and order from those dashing doors..."

"DoorDash, granny," he clowned and got out to hug her too.

While we stood on her front lawn and chatted, the last of the emergency vehicles left until the block was cleared. "So, do you feel alright going back into your house after all that stuff happened?" Quinton asked.

"Shit, it wasn't like there was blood or anything. He just closed his eyes and din never open 'em again. All I gotta do is go inside and change the sheets. I think I can handle that all by myself. The only thing that had me shook was going to jail because I killed Robert. Now that I know that I'm not, I'm good."

"Granny!"

"What? I'm serious. Who knew the coochie could be used as a weapon? I mean... I feel bad for his passing, but it ain't like I was in love with him or like he left me some big insurance policy. He gave me what he came over for and I'm good."

"Granny!"

There was no talking to his grandmother and there was no stopping me from crying real tears of laughter. The shit was hilarious.

"Hush, Q. Thanks for coming, but I'm okay. You just enjoy your night out with your new wife, and we'll plan something next week or something."

After we left there, it still took me another five minutes to stop laughing. It may have been heartless because a life was lost, but I couldn't help it. His cause of death was killing me. Literally!

"Who is this now?" Quinton complained when his cell rang soon as we jumped on the highway heading home. "Shawn! Fuck!"

As he answered it, I tried to tune him out but the hollering coming from the other end prevented it. "This bitch is crazy!"

"Deal with that shit when you touch back down. Just concentrate on the dough right now and let me know if I can do anything on my end."

If it wasn't one thing, it was another and by the way the evening was turning out, it didn't look like sex was going to remain on the menu. At least no time soon...

Chapter Eight

Shawn Fulcher

"That stressed me the hell out when Quinton ran off to Vegas and left me in Houston to run the crew. Shit, after that, a nigga needed a working vacation away from them fools."

"I thought he said nobody knew where he went?" Rachel blurted out.

"I know all about his moves. Q always keeps me in the loop."

"Oh, he does, huh?" she taunted like she knew something that I didn't know, but how? What?

Being the curious dude I was, I played the hell out of her until I had her blabbing that Quinton married Justice when he was down there. It shocked me so badly that I had to bite my tongue to stop myself from asking a million questions.

"I couldn't believe he did that shit, and I really can't believe he told you. What's up between y'all that he would trust you with some shit like that?"

"He posted it on social media," Rachel revealed.

"Oh, yea! I don't have that shit, but Doreen did tell me about it," I continued to lie as I sat at the red light with my mind blown.

Damn this nigga really went and married Justice? After he had me and Jimmy murk her mama? That nigga was playing with fire, and I didn't want to be there when that muthafucka got burned.

Maybe it was good that he sent me up here to San Antonio with Rachel. This bitch was running her mouth about everything and everybody. Like she was the baddest bitch from our hood, and it only got worse each time one of our clients flirted with her. Her head was getting bigger by the day.

Even though I didn't much care for her cocky attitude, I couldn't lie; Rachel was clocking her dough. Her tips alone were more than what Quinton had me paying her. That was what had her motivated.

If she kept that shit up, by the time we were ready to leave San Antonio, she would be bringing home five figures easily. Women had it so much easier than men.

"You hungry?" I asked Rachel after we left the last spot.

"I am. What do you feel like eating?"

"What I feel like eating can't be found on anybody's menu," I flirted.

"HA! Not trying to hear that shit from you, so pump your brakes Papi," she said as she threw her hand up in my face as I drove onto the main highway. "Whatever you feeling down there, please keep it to yourself."

"Why you always think I'm offering you some of this?"

"Cuz you are!"

"No, I'm not!" I lied.

"You don't think I know you want some of me?" Rachel clowned with too much confidence for me.

"I already got a girl!"

"What girl? I know you ain't talking about Doreen! Cuz, I heard she moved on."

Now why the fuck was this girl playing with me right now? Doreen hadn't moved on. She was just toying with that dude at the club. Doreen knew that I was out there fucking with other females, so she wanted to make me jealous. It was cool though because I had my own shit going on anyway.

"Good if she moved on because I wasn't even talking about her. Hell, me and Doreen been done. Done- done!"

"Okay, cool. Since you weren't talking about yo baby mama and you insist you gotta chick, then we should be able to work without you shooting your shots at me and shit!"

"I really don't know why the hell you keep saying I'm shooting shots at you cuz I ain't fired one shot your way! I barely wanna work with yo ass, so what the hell I look like trying to fuck you!"

"Kiss my ass, Shawn! I know what it feels like when a dude is trying to hit on me, and you've been doing that since we been out here," she countered.

"Don't flatter yo'self! Truth be told, you ain't even that cute!" I fired back. "Now ya girl Justice... yea, if she wasn't married to my boy Quinton, she could get it!"

Rachel's face twisted up in a scowl that had her looking like a hardened criminal. And she had me ready to die laughing. That was what I called 'flipping the script'. She was trying to piss me off but ended up getting pissed off. That was what the fuck she got for trying to clown me.

"What's the matter? You mad now?" I teased with a chuckle.

"Just get me back to the hotel please so I can get the fuck away from you!"

I could tell in her voice that she was really mad. It wasn't my intention to piss her off like that because we still had to work together, but she played herself. There was no way she was going to make an ass out of me and get away with it.

"Don't be mad! You started this shit, so you should have known I would have finished it."

"Don't fuckin' talk to me no more unless it's about business!" she snapped as she stared out the window.

"I can do that if you quit thinking I'm trying to fuck yo ass! Lemme make that clear, I don't want you! If we weren't here doing business, I wouldn't be in the same room with you at all," I stated in a matter of fact tone.

Now, don't get me wrong, if she had offered the pussy, I might have taken it. But to say I was going to keep pursuing her like I did my baby mama, fuck that!

Like I said, Rachel wasn't all that anyway. She had a nice body on her, and her face was cute, but she was the type that the more you drank, the better she looked. I wanted a bad bitch! Not a bitch I had to get drunk to want.

"I'm glad we're clear on where we stand," Rachel said.

"Shit, I been clear!"

After I barked that shit at her, she didn't say anything else, and that was fine with me. Since she wanted to act like a bitch, she could find her way around to get her own fucking dinner!

"I think you can understand why I won't be eating with yo ass, right?" I asked as I looked over at her briefly.

"That's fine with me! I can find my own way around San Antonio. It ain't my first time coming here!" she stated as she crossed her arms over her chest.

While she was steadily talking shit, I pulled up to the hotel and waited for her to get out. When she finally did, that bitch had the nerve to slam my fucking door as hard as she could. This wasn't no rental.

This was my own personal ride, so she was lucky I didn't get out and go off on her fucking ass for banging my door shut like that. If she pulled some disrespectful shit like that again, I was going to make her ass find another way home tomorrow. Even if she didn't, I was still thinking about sticking her ass in the backseat, or maybe even the damn trunk. It all depended on what type of mood I was in at the time.

"Bitch!" I hissed through the closed window.

After Rachel stormed off, I hit up Quinton to tell him about her ass, but he seemed to be too busy to listen to what I had to say. Like what the hell could be more important than me wanting to kill this bitch who put to work with me? I wished that he would have chosen someone else to babysit that broad!

As I shook my head at all the bullshit, I pulled off from the hotel and headed to the Riverwalk. Whenever I came out here, that was my favorite place to visit. The people were friendly, and the food was always on point. Not to mention the good music. It constantly set the ambiance in every restaurant.

This visit, I decided to eat at Dick's Last Resort because I wanted some American food. They had everything on their menu from hamburgers and hot dogs to ribs and chicken. Might as well indulge in what I was used to. After being seated and placing my order, I watched the action going on in the water. There were gondola boats with happy couples riding in them.

"Those were some good times," I mumbled under my breath as I sat there waiting for my food.

As I got lost in my thoughts, I remembered me and Doreen coming to San Antonio before she had Laya.

We had so much fun during that time. I wanted to do everything I could with her just to show her how much I loved her. We went on a gondola boat and sat close together as the driver steered us around the Riverwalk.

By the time we got off the boat, I was ready for some good loving. I took her upstairs to our hotel room where we soaked in a tub of warm bubbled water together. After we were done, I was ready to get busy, but my girl was hungry, so we ordered room service.

After we ate, I was finally able to put this dick on her. I tore that pussy up that night and for the next three nights. By the time we made it back home to Houston, we were more in love than before we left. Only thing was during the time we were gone, we had created a baby.

I wasn't trippin' about that shit though because I loved Doreen. What could be better than having a baby with the woman I knew I wanted to spend the rest of my life with? I thought the two of us having a baby would only bring us closer together. That did not happen.

After Doreen gave birth, we were good for the first two years, but with the job that I did, bitches threw the pussy at me from time to time. Me and Doreen started getting into it because she was accusing me of shit, I wasn't even doing. When a nigga got accused of shit, he wasn't doing, he might as well do it.

I mean, she already thought I was fucking so I started fucking other hoes. Then when she found out, she decided she wanted a fucking break. How the hell she wanted a break now that I was fucking? She didn't want a break before when she was throwing around accusations.

When she packed her shit and left, I wanted to tell her not to leave with my daughter, but in an effort to not argue or fight in front of Laya, I let them go.

"Daddy will see you soon, Laya," I assured my baby girl.

"Don't make promises you can't keep," Doreen said.

"Oh, trust me when I say, I will see my daughter. If you or anyone think you can keep us apart, you better think again," I threatened.

"Whatever boy!" she scoffed.

It wasn't that I didn't love Doreen, but once she found out that I had cheated, the trust was gone. After that, we couldn't seem to get along. I didn't like all that arguing around our daughter. She didn't deserve that at all. What Laya deserved were two parents who were going to do their best to make sure that she came first.

We had to put our feelings for each other aside and think about our daughter. I could be mature enough to do that, but my baby mama was childish as fuck! I missed my child every day that we were apart, but not enough to go back to the way things were with her mom before I left.

At first, Doreen made it hard as fuck for me to see my child. It was like she wanted to keep us apart for whatever selfish reason she had, and I didn't like that shit at all. I had been there from day one when Laya entered the world, so I was sure that as much as I missed her, she missed me too. The bond between a child and parent couldn't be broken no matter how badly people tried to do just that.

Finally, after a week of keeping my daughter from me, Doreen let me come over for a visit. "Bout time!" I stated as I walked into the apartment.

"Don't get slick at the mouth nigga, cuz you will find your ass right back on the other side of this door!" she threatened.

I didn't want to argue with her because that was what she wanted. She wanted the two of us to get into it so she would have a valid reason to throw me out on my ass. So, I wasn't going to give her one.

As soon as my baby girl saw me, she rushed over to me with her arms in the air. "Da-yeeeee!!" she cried with joy. I lifted her up in my arms and just held her close for a good ten minutes. After that, she was struggling with me to let go, which was funny to me.

"Daddy missed you so much, baby," I whined. "You miss daddy?"

"Yeah!"

"Well, if daddy wouldn't have been such an ass, we would all be together," Doreen said which caused Laya to look at me sideways. She was most likely trying to understand what her mom was saying, which wasn't doing either of us any good.

I didn't even give her the satisfaction of pissing me off. I just rolled my eyes at her and kept my attention focused on my baby girl. I sat on the sofa and chatted with Laya while she sat on my lap.

She leaned her head against my chest. "Daddy loves you so much baby girl. You have no idea how lonely I've been without you this past week," I admitted.

"Daddy loves you so much," Doreen mocked in an arrogant tone. "I've been so lonely and miserable without you," she continued as she made weird faces and rolled her eyes dramatically.

She was lucky that I was here for Laya because if I wasn't, I would have for sure given her a piece of mind that she wouldn't forget anytime soon. The games that she was playing regarding our daughter wasn't cool.

"Don't you have something else you would rather be doing?" I asked.

"You mean something more important than supervising my child's visit with her daddy... hell no!"

"Supervise!" I barked while trying to blow my cap. "I don't need nobody hanging around to "supervise" me girl! I'm a grown ass man and in case you forgot, I've been Laya's dad for the past two years! I been helping yo ass take care of our daughter, so trust me when I say, I know what the hell I'm doing!"

"I didn't say you didn't know. I'd just prefer to sit here than do anything else," she replied snidely. "And please watch what you say in front of our child!"

"But it's okay for you to say what you want in front of her though. And why the heck are you acting like I'm one of those sex offender fathers that need supervised visits!" I stated. "I know how to take care of my baby!"

"Yea, okay."

I sat on the floor with Laya, and she immediately grabbed some toys for us to play with. I definitely indulged in doing that with her for about three hours. The whole time I sat with my daughter, Doreen sat on the sofa making noises that let me know she wanted me to leave. But since I was here for Laya, I blocked out my baby mama and her childish attitude.

Me and my little girl enjoyed ourselves for the rest of the afternoon and by the time I left, she was good and tired. It was around five that evening, and I almost didn't want to leave my little girl, but I couldn't wait to get away from her mom.

She made me feel so uncomfortable while I was there, and I figured that was what she had aimed to do. As I made my way to the door, Doreen followed behind me, all the way outside the apartment.

"Where is Laya?" I asked.

"With Frankie! DUH!"

"Frankie has been here the whole time?"

"That's what I just said," she replied with a smart attitude.

I shook my head. "Wow! So, instead of watching me all afternoon, you could have been chillin' with your friend in her room," I said.

"I didn't wanna chill with her."

"Well, I'm not gonna be visiting here like that just cuz that's the way you want it. I should be able to keep my daughter at my house. Shit, she spent the first two years of her life there, so I don't see what the problem is."

"I just don't want my child away from me..."

"Now, that's dumb as fuck! I'm her dad, and I would never hurt her, so you having to be with us every time with we visit ain't gonna work for me," I said.

"Well, you don't get to decide that!" she stated.

"I bet the fuck I do! Don't make me get a lawyer and fight yo ass in court cuz I will."

"Wow! Really!"

"Fuckin' right! My name is on the birth certificate too, so that gives me just as many rights as yo ass! Fight me on it if you want to but you will lose!"

Thankfully, that was enough to scare her ass and we were able to come up with a visitation schedule that was good for everyone... until now. We were currently back at square one because I had allowed Syanna to watch Laya for a little while. I was trying to give Doreen some space and time to cool off, but I wasn't going to play that game with her much longer.

When I got back home, she was going to have to let me see my daughter. Otherwise, we were going to have a fight on our hands.

As my mind continued to wander, I actually started to miss Doreen a little. At least if she was here with me, I wouldn't be going to bed alone tonight. I would be going to the hotel getting some good ass head.

Doreen was the best at that shit...

Chapter Nine

Doreen Collins

Ugh, I had enough of Shawn's attitude and demanding ways, but it didn't matter how badly he treated me, I still loved his ass. For example, that night I saw him dancing with that bitch at the club.

That shit was still running me hot. I didn't even know my baby daddy was in the club when I was throwing my ass on my friend Jamison. If I had, I surely wouldn't have been doing no shit like that. Not even to make him jealous. Truthfully, I was just having a good time.

Now, Shawn, on the other hand... he was definitely trying to piss me off when he started dancing with that bitch with the big muscular arms. I didn't know how he even found her attractive when her arms were bigger than his. What kind of sense did that even make?

Ever since that unfair fight, me and Shawn had been arguing. I couldn't believe he let that bitch fight me then called himself trying to leave with her. That shit right there showed me how disloyal he was to me and our daughter. So, while he was thinking that I was keeping Laya away from him because I was salty about losing that battle with that *She Hulk*, I wasn't. I was pissed because he showed me that he didn't have my back.

That shit was foul and if Shawn wasn't going to be the man that I needed him to be, he wasn't the man for me. Sadly, he showed me he wasn't that night.

It didn't matter if we were still with each other or not, we had a daughter together. Instead of turning his back on me, he should've been protecting me, especially after all that I had done for him. All the passes I had given to him. Hell, the baby I birthed for him, and that was how he wanted to do me!

Shawn literally gave me his ass to kiss in front of everyone, including my best friend, Frankie. I was mad and humiliated. There was no way we could ever come back from what happened at the club.

Now I had two bitches on my hit list... that Syanna ho' and Ashleigh, the bitch from Marvel comics.

No lie though, I had been going to the gym three times a week since me and that heifer got into it. I needed to get my muscles intact because I was going to fight that ho' again, and next time, I'd be ready for that battle. There was no way I would lose that fight!

In my mind, Ashleigh was not going to have a chance because I was going to come at her swinging like Tyson before she even knew who or what was coming at her. As for sleezy Syanna, I wasn't even worried about her trick ass because I sure had something for her.

"Aren't you tired fighting bitches for Shawn?" Frankie asked.

"I'm not fighting no bitch for Shawn!"

"You sure about that?" she asked as she side eyed me.

"I'm positive. What the hell I look like fighting a bitch for a nigga I didn't want anymore?" I questioned.

"Oh, you can sit here and lie to me and to yourself because I know for a fact that you still want him, Doreen. What I don't understand is why though when he disrespects you every chance he gets. I remember when y'all first got together and Shawn used to treat you like his queen. These days, he treats you like a side chick instead of his baby mama," Frankie continued.

As much pain as it caused me to hear my best friend say that to me, she was right. I had no idea what happened between me and Shawn to make him do me like that, but he had definitely changed, and not for the better either.

"Ain't nobody thinking about fighting over Shawn. I done told you that a dozen times."

"Then why are you wasting your time training yourself to fight that bitch from the club again? Just let that shit go D!"

"Let it go! Did you say let it go?" I asked.

"What are we part of the *Frozen* cartoon now?" Frankie asked.

"I'm not laughing Frankie! Damn! Did you not see how she punked me that night? I don't care whose nigga she fucks with, when she fucked with me, she fucked with the wrong bitch. I'm getting her back. It's not a love thing. It's a pride thing. I can't just let her get away with getting me like that at the club. I gotta get her back."

"I saw, but you won't win every fight D! Sometimes you will lose. That doesn't mean that you have to go another round with a bitch cuz you lost!" Frankie argued. "That's dumb!"

"You calling me dumb!" I asked feeling insulted.

"I'm not calling you dumb. I'm saying it's dumb for you to want to fight a chick again just cuz she already beat you. What's the point of revisiting that shit?"

"Because she beat my ass in front of all my damn friends! People who know and saw that shit are still laughing at me!" I repeated for the third damn time.

"Fuck them people! You have a daughter D! She's the only one you should be worried about," Frankie countered.

"I don't worry about my daughter because she's taken care of. People who worry about their children do that because they don't take care of their babies," I said.

"Uh huh."

Frankie was getting on my nerves so badly right now that I had to change the subject before we ended up fighting. Something that we had never done.

"Have you spoken to your man today?" I asked.

"Yea. Why?"

"Did he mention Shawn?"

Right away, Frankie covered her face with her hand and blew out a breath. For some reason, she was losing her patience with me, but I bet she wouldn't say that.

Me and Frankie had been best friends all these years for a reason. I was a hot head, but she was more levelheaded. We balanced each other very well, but sometimes, she still worked my nerves and managed to drive me insane.

"You know I don't like to get in the middle of y'all shit, Doreen," she grunted and frowned up. "Just because we're best friends and we're dating brothers doesn't mean that I can tell you everything

Square tells me, especially when he shares shit about his brother in confidence. That's gonna cause problems in my relationship and I ain't with that."

"So, to hell with it if it fucks up mine, right?"

"From what you just said, you and Shawn's relationship is already fucked up." Frankie clowned. "And it been fucked up!"

"We have a daughter together though," I argued.

"And that means what exactly?"

"That if it affects me or Laya, I need to know."

"Well, it doesn't. Y'all both here and y'all both cool."

"So, Shawn's not here? He's out of town?" I asked wondering why the fuck he ain't tell me he was gone. How the hell Square and Frankie knew, but I didn't? That was fucked all the way up!

Ugh, I hated to be the last to know shit about Shawn, especially when it was my best friend who knew first. Whether Frankie knew she was rubbing it in my face or not, she needed to tell me what she knew. If she didn't, I guess that meant we weren't as close as I thought we were.

Hell, if I knew something about Square, I would tell her in a heartbeat. Why was it so different with Frankie telling me about Shawn? I didn't understand.

"Just tell me, Frankie. What is it?"

"What is what?"

Now she wanted to act like she didn't know what I was talking about. *Ain't that a bitch?*

The longer she played dumb, the more upset I became. If she didn't break down soon and spill the beans, I was ready to shake it out of her. That was how frustrated she had me.

"Frankie, where is he? Where is Shawn?"

"Look, if I tell you, you ain't gonna do nothing but run and call him. When you do, he's gonna know his brother told me and I told you. That shit right there is gonna cause a bunch of problems between Shawn and Square, then between me and Square, and finally, me and you."

"Me and you?" I shrieked with a raised brow.

"Yes, because I'm gonna be mad at you for going back and running your mouth. The last five damn times I told you something that Square told me about Shawn, you ran right back and told."

"I didn't tell him who told me."

"Doreen, you ain't have to. Shawn knows the only person that knew his business was his brother. Stop it."

"Look, are you gonna tell me or not, Frankie?"

Yes, I was putting the pressure on her. That little ugly face she was making didn't matter at all. The only thing that mattered to me was where Shawn was and who the hell he was with.

That's it. That's all.

"Ugh!"

"Ugh, my ass, Frankie. If you are really my fucking friend, you would just tell me what I need to know instead of making me beg you for information."

"I am your friend and that's why I don't wanna tell you."

"So, are you worried that what you're gonna tell me is gonna hurt my feelings? Because if you are, you're sadly mistaken. Shawn and I are on a break from each other, so he is free to do what he wants. I just wanna know," I lied.

"Fuck it, Doreen! I'm gonna tell you this last time and if you run back and tell this shit, I'm done. I swear! I ain't gonna tell you nothing else, so don't even ask. I'm so serious! I can walk into the house over there and catch him fucking ten bitches and I'm not gonna say shit. So, it's on you. Make the choice."

"I know you fucking lying, Frankie. If you saw Shawn fucking another chick best believe you had better record it for proof! Or even better, FaceTime me so I can see for myself," I teased to lighten the mood.

As Frankie laughed along with me, she blurted out that Shawn was in San Antonio. Before I could ask her what he was doing there and who he was with, she told me that he was there with Rachel, but assured me that it was strictly business.

"Rachel Gwinn?!" I yelled ready to drive up there and fuck them both up.

"Yes, and before you go off, Quinton sent them up there together to handle some shit. Shawn's mad and feels like he's babysitting, so I highly doubt that they're messing around."

"Shit, the babysitter fucks their employees all the time, so that don't mean a damn thing!" I scoffed.

Beyond upset and embarrassed yet again, I was ready to dial Shawn's number. The only reason why I didn't was because I didn't want to prove that Frankie was right.

Oh, that didn't mean I wouldn't hop on social media and reach out to Rachel's grimy ass though. All I wanted to know was if she was fucking my baby daddy or not. For her sake, she had better give me the right answer. Because if she didn't, I would be on the highway, locked, loaded and ready to hunt their asses down. They could try me if they wanted to...

Chapter Ten

Rachel Gwinn

First Shawn wanted to act a fool because a bitch wasn't giving him no play. What the hell did he think it was gon be like? That just because we were out of town together it was going to be on and cracking!

No, we were in San Antonio on business and that was where my mind was. More than ever, I was focused and determined to make enough money to take care of myself. I wanted to show Quinton that he lost out on a good thing.

Forget what he was talking about. I was a fucking prize and if he couldn't see that before, he was about to see it real soon. I was about to go back and hustle even harder just so I could shit on all of them. Anyone who ever doubted me.

As I boosted my confidence, I walked up to the two- bedroom suite that Quinton rented for me and Shawn. Once closed in, I ordered myself some food since that nigga wanted to act shady. Like I couldn't get my own fucking food. I wasn't a damn child who had to wait for my parents to feed me. I knew how to take the steps to order my own damn food!

While I waited on my food to arrive, I went to shower and change. Today had been a long, but profitable day, so I couldn't complain about it.

All that changed when I went to the door, got my food, tipped the guy really good only to find out the shit was nasty as hell. Pissed me off!

"This is some straight bullshit!" I grunted as I went to grab my cell off the table.

Just as I went to pull up the app to see how to get a refund, I got several alerts on my main social media page. Curious to find out who was getting at me, I quickly hopped online and opened up my inbox.

"What the fuck?" I smirked when I saw Doreen's profile pic pop up.

Why the hell was she wearing that same old tired weave? She was cute, but she needed to switch that ugly ass shit, change the color or something.

"What could she possibly want?"

Before I opened her messages, I went to get a shot bottle of Jack from the minibar and downed it then opened a second one. As I went to sit on the sofa to read what Doreen had sent, I almost choked. Was this bitch serious?

"Ain't nobody fucking her man. Don't nobody want that loose muthafucka but her ass. I don't care how fine he is. His reputation fucks all that up," I said to myself as my inbox started ringing.

Did this bold bitch really call me through messenger? Who did that silly shit?

"Let me answer this before she keeps calling me. I need to set this straight right now."

"How may I help you, Doreen?" I greeted without allowing the video to show.

All I needed was this crazy chick to see I was in a hotel room if she did indeed know I was in San Antonio with Shawn. Like I said, it was business.

"What's up with you being out of town with my baby daddy? Is there something going on between y'all that I need to know about?"

"Doreen, first of all, I'm trying to figure out why you are even calling me right now. Second, that's hella childish for you to be calling me through this app! If you need answers concerning your baby daddy Shawn, you need to call him... not me! I ain't got time for all that!"

"Are you fucking him, or no? Just answer the question..."

"What?" I gasped. This bitch was bolder than I thought to be coming at me like that.

"ARE YOU FUCKING SHAWN, MY BABY DADDY?!" Doreen hollered in my ear. "Can you hear me now?!"

"Girl bye! You act like yo nigga is Morris Chestnut or somebody fine! Don't nobody want that muthafucka like that but you!" I cracked as I busted out laughing. "The only thing I'm doing with yo baby daddy is getting this paper. If you ain't cool with that, take it up with him or Quinton!"

"Where is Shawn?"

"Shit, how the hell should I know. Like I told you, this is a business trip, and I'm in my room."

"So, y'all got separate rooms?" Doreen continued to question me as if she didn't hear me say MY room. This bitch was really pushing it and after just getting into an argument with Shawn's triflin' ass, I was more irritated than before.

"Doreen, listen to me and listen good. I'm not fucking yo man, yo baby daddy or whoever he is to you. If that ain't good enough..."

Soon as I got that last word out, in walked Shawn. He just came busting in the door talking shit like I gave a damn about his business. It was too late to tell him to pipe down because Doreen had already heard him.

"Put that muthafucka on the phone right now!" she demanded.

She was so loud that Shawn heard her and shut the hell up. While he was dancing around whispering questions my way, I was shaking my head.

It was either hang up or put him on the phone. Now, the choice was his.

Without saying a word, I held my cell towards him. Shawn immediately shook his head, 'no'. That left me to politely hit the red icon.

"What the fuck, Rachel? You was that mad that you had to call my baby mama and start some shit!"

"Okay, first of all, watch your tone when you speaking to me!"

"I ain't gotta watch shit! Especially if you out here starting shit between me and my fuckin' baby mama!" he stated.

"Boy bye! Ain't nobody worried about you or your baby mama! Look at this! Look at my inbox and you will see that she's the one who called me!"

"Why the hell would she call you?" I asked.

"That's something you will have to ask her! Why the hell would I call her when I know how crazy she is?"

"Well, why the fuck she call you?"

"Like I said, you need to ask her that!"

"How the hell she knows where I am or that we're together?" Shawn pressed nervously as Doreen called me through messenger over and over.

"How the hell would I know that shit, Shawn? I didn't have a chance to tell her."

"What *did* you have a chance to tell her, Rachel?"

"Well, I was just telling her that we weren't fucking and that I definitely ain't sharing a room with you... but you kinda fucked that up when you busted in the room yelling like you didn't have any damn sense. That's your own fault, Shawn." I laughed as I opened my third shot bottle of Jack.

"How is it my fault? And stop fucking drinking! You ain't even old enough to drink!"

"Really. You wanna police me now?" I asked as I side eyed him. "I got an ID that says I'm twenty-one..."

"Please don't start waving around that fake ID Quinton gets for everybody. You ain't special!"

"And neither are you," I clowned. "Now call yo baby mama back before she drives up here and find us before Tuesday. And have her stop calling my damn phone! Shit, what's today?"

Soon as Shawn told me what day it was, I felt bad for not calling Justice earlier. It was finally her eighteenth birthday.

Now ignoring him, I picked up my cell and called my best friend three times before I gave up and left a message singing happy birthday to her. As I silently wondered what Justice was doing, Shawn was pacing the living room floor of the suite while he dialed Doreen.

All I could do was sit there and laugh as the two of them went at it. I could hear her big ass mouth from across the room. She was talking big mess about me, and it really didn't bother me until she called me a nasty ho. She even said I had fucked almost every nigga in the hood.

"Ask the ho and I bet she tell you." Doreen shouted out.

"Tell her to leave my name out her fuckin' mouth! I ain't done shit to her, but I can," I said flirting with Shawn.

Did I like him? Hell no! But I may have been drunk enough to fuck him just to get back at his baby mama. She was way out of line for making that comment about me. I wasn't the type of female to be giving my goodies to everybody the way she was saying. The fucking nerve!

"Yo, why you gotta play like that?!" Shawn hissed angrily, but I kept right on laughing.

That alcohol I drank certainly gave me more courage than I realized because before I knew it, Doreen and I were arguing. It wasn't until she threatened to shoot me that I snapped out of it.

"Say what?"

"Bitch, you ain't gonna be in San Antonio forever! You gotta come back to Houston some time and when you do, that ass is mine!" Doreen warned.

"Ain't shit going on between us so cut that shit out!" Shawn fussed. "I just came to her room to cash her out..."

"Nigga, you went in there a little too cheery for me and that bitch over there drunk too! You don't think I hear her slurring and shit, Shawn?" Doreen yelled through the phone.

"Look, I'm about to go back to my room and call you. I'm not about to stand here in this girl's room going at it with you."

"No, if you ain't fucking that bitch, then send for me. Or tell me where you're staying so I can come up there..."

"By the time you do all that, I'll be on my way home. Now, I'm about to hang up and holla back at you in a second."

Shawn disconnected the call and looked at me before he questioned me again. Didn't he hear me the first time? Shit, he was messing up my buzz.

"I ain't call her!"

"She gonna fuck you up when you get back and that's gon be on you. You wanna sit up here and argue with her when you know she ain't scared to go to jail, Rachel."

"I ain't worried about fighting that girl," I lied.

"Well, if you gonna fight her, you may as well have a reason," Shawn flirted as he licked his lips.

Damn, if I wasn't so addicted to Quinton, I would have fucked him just on GP. Just because his baby mama was so disrespectful, but no. I wasn't sleeping with nobody except for my boo, Q. Nobody could satisfy me but him. That I was sure of.

"Get outta here and go to your room to call Doreen before she comes looking for you."

"You mean, before she comes looking for us?" Shawn chuckled as his phone rang.

"Shit, she ain't gotta come looking for me," I mumbled.

I would've talked some more shit, but before I could, he was running off to his room like a little bitch. How was he gonna be scared of his baby mama? Punk!

Now that he was out of my hair, I could enjoy one last drink before I went to lay down and call Quinton again. Knowing I was blocked, and I would have to go through Shawn if I needed to speak to him didn't stop me from trying.

"Damn, why this nigga dodging me like that?" I whined to myself. "He knows I hate when he does that shit!"

If he would just fuck with me, I wouldn't tell Justice anything. She was my friend, but that was just how much I loved Quinton. If only he could see that shit.

"My boo," I chanted as I looked at his picture on my phone.

My eyes were so glued to it that I put myself into a deep daze until I finally drifted off and had me a nice little dream about Quinton. Just when it started to get too good, it got too real.

"Muthafucka!" I hollered as I tried to roll Shawn up off me.

Was he insane for coming in my room and trying to sneak the pussy? Did he think I was that drunk?

Well, whatever he thought, he had a rude awakening when I reached under my pillow and whipped out my knife. Shawn didn't know what was coming for him until he was sliced down the cheek. Oh, that muthafucka got off me then.

"You fucking bastard! How dare you!" I yelled as I noticed that my shorts were gone, and my tank was off one of my shoulders. Titties hanging out and everything.

"Bitch, you fuckin' cut me!" Shawn hollered.

"Nigga you lucky that was all I did to you! You tried to rape me!"

"Bitch please! What the fuck I look like trying to rape yo ass?" he questioned which angered me even more.

"Well, what the hell you call it? You got my clothes almost off and shit!" I yelled.

"I ain't tried to rape you, girl! Shit, I knocked on the fuckin' door, and you said come in. When I did and heard you in here moaning and groaning while playing with yourself, I just joined in. The way you pulled me against you and shit, I thought you was into it!"

"I wasn't into shit! Nigga, are you crazy?"

"Well, you sure didn't stop me..."

"Oh, but I bet my knife did though!" I snapped as I got off the bed and held it out towards him to show that I wasn't playing.

"Bitch, I swear, if I gotta get stitches..."

"Stitches will be the least of your worries if you step to me sideways again, Shawn. I'm not playing with yo ass! You'll be a dead nigga, and somebody will have to come to San Antonio to identify your damn body! Try me!"

"Yo ass just as crazy as my baby mama! I ain't fooling with you, Rachel. I swear, if I thought it wouldn't fuck up business, I would shoot yo ass where you stand..."

"Just get out, Shawn!" I yelled.

As he left my room and closed the door behind him, I breathed in deeply as my body shook with fear. That fool had lost his damn mind.

And almost his life!

Chapter Eleven

Quinton Marshall

Although Justice's birthday didn't go quite the way I planned because of her upset stomach then my grandmother's drama, it got a whole lot better at dinner. At the nice upscale soul food restaurant, we were able to enjoy a delicious meal while discussing our future.

Then when we made it back home and had a few cocktails, I carried Justice upstairs and prepared to get romantic. My plan probably would've worked if I had remembered to cut off my cell. That bad boy was ringing nonstop. What the hell?

"It's pretty late, Q, so whoever is calling you like that must be doing it because it's important," Justice whined then busted out laughing. "It may be your grandmother again..."

"Don't even clown like that!" I chuckled as I picked up my phone and frowned when I looked at the screen. "What this nigga want now?"

The only thing that made me answer was business. If something was seriously wrong, I would want to know about it ASAP.

"What's up? Everything good?" I checked.

"Nigga, this bitch just cut me!" Shawn fussed.

He was yelling so loud that I had to step out of the room to talk to him. "What?! Who the fuck cut you?"

"Rachel, that bitch cut me! Sliced me in the fucking face with a blade and shit! Got me over here at the hospital getting stitches. I swear I'm about to murk that..."

As much as he would be doing me a huge favor, I couldn't bring myself to let him do that. Rachel hadn't done me dirty, so I had no reason to kill her. What she did to Shawn was on him though. It was confirmed when he explained what happened.

Shit, he shouldn't have been in Rachel's room to begin with. He was damn lucky that she didn't have her heater. She would've surely killed his ass.

Truthfully, I would've been partially to blame seeing that I was the one who booked their room. To maybe fuck so Rachel could leave me alone. Not for her to try to dead Shawn. Damn!

"Aight nigga, calm down! The last thing I need is for you to go rogue on me!" I stated.

"Did you hear what the fuck I said? That bitch sliced my damn face!"

"Sir I'm gonna need you to hang up the phone so we can stitch your wound," the nurse said.

"I gotta go, but you better handle that bitch cuz if I do it, you might not like how that shit ends," Shawn warned.

"I'm about to call her," I told him.

"You better do something!"

After Shawn hung the phone up on me, I hit up Rachel. She answered on the first ring. "Thank God you called!"

"Yo, what the hell going on out there? I sent you niggas out there for business purposes..."

"Tell that to ya boy! He's the one who came in my bedroom and started taking off my clothes!"

"He said you told him to come in," I explained.

"I don't remember that shit!" she slurred.

"Well, considering you been killing the drinks from the minibar in your suite, you may not remember."

"Are you saying this is my fault?" Rachel asked.

"I'm saying that you invited him in, so you shouldn't have been surprised the way things played out," I enlightened.

"The fucking nerve..."

"Watch your fuckin' tone yo! You know I don't play that shit!" I warned.

"Sorry, but I have a problem with you accusing me of shit I didn't do."

"I didn't accuse you of shit, but I know Shawn and he ain't the type of nigga to just invade your space like that!"

"And you know me!"

"I also know that you're drunk! Sometimes when you're under the influence, it clouds your brain. I'm sure Shawn didn't mean to come at you the way you claim that he did, but when you invite a nigga into your room while you fondling yourself, what the fuck you think gon happen?"

"Is everything okay Quinton?" Justice asked.

"Yea babe. Gimme two more minutes and I'll be right there," I said.

"Okay. Don't keep me waiting on you too long."

"Shit, never that babe," I teased with a wink.

"Really! Did you forget that I was on the phone?"

"No, but you do know I'm married, right? So, hearing Justice's voice in the background shouldn't come as any surprise to you," I stated.

"I'm not surprised that she's there considering your fucking union and all. I just didn't expect you to not take my feelings into consideration just now..."

"I'm not worried about your feelings Rachel. I don't mean to sound insensitive to you..."

"Well, that's exactly how you sound!" she whined.

"Look, I need you and Shawn to do the job I sent y'all out there to do. With that being said, stop sipping that sauce and slicing that nigga! You shouldn't be drinking none of that shit in the fucking minibar cuz that ain't why you are there!"

"What's the fucking point of having an ID that allows me to be grown if I can't drink?"

"Do the fucking job I sent you there to do! Don't make me have to repeat myself again!" I spoke through clenched teeth. "Got it?"

"Yea, I got it. Do me a favor and don't fuck my friend!" She sniffled.

"The fuck you just said?"

"Don't fuck Justice!"

"Girl bye! I ain't about to fuck my wife, especially since it's her first time. I am about to take my time and gently make love to her though. I mean, since you wanna be all up in our fucking business and shit!" I stated with a chuckle. "I bet you wish you had kept that comment to yourself huh?"

As I waited to hear what else Rachel had to say, I got nothing but silence for the next few seconds. Then came all that fucking sobbing. Did I feel bad for her? I supposed, but I wasn't that kind of nigga.

"Enjoy the rest of your night, Rachel."

She didn't bother saying anything. She just hung the phone up, and that was fine with me because what I didn't want was someone on my line whining like a baby.

To make sure I didn't get any more unnecessary interruptions, I walked back in the room, turned my phone off then placed it on the charger. With a sense of satisfaction, I looked over at Justice who was laying on her side in the bed with an elbow propped up on a pillow.

The black lace negligee she wore had my dick about to bust out my pajama bottom. It was hard as hell to keep it concealed.

"Everything okay?" Justice inquired.

"Yep," I answered as I climbed in bed and made my way over to her. "Just some bullshit with work."

"Sounded serious."

"Nothing they can't handle themselves. I don't wanna think or worry about them anymore. All I wanna concentrate on right now is you. Did you enjoy your birthday today?" I inquired as I settled my head on the pillow next to her.

"I did, and I owe it all to you. You know when I woke up this morning, I didn't think that I would have a good day," she confessed.

"No? Why not?"

"Because this is the first birthday without my mom," she confessed as she lowered her head sadly.

"I'm sorry your mom ain't here for your special day," I replied as my heart tightened with guilt.

"I know a lot of people feel like I shouldn't be so sad that she's not here because of the way she took care of me. But I understood my mom's addiction, and I dealt with it. I knew that she tried her best to do what she could for me, so I can't fault her for that. My grandmother passed when my mom was only fifteen, and she had been taking care of herself ever since..." She stopped talking and brushed a tear away.

"I didn't know that."

"Yea, how could you if she didn't share it with you? My mom didn't wanna be put in the foster care system because she was pregnant with me. She didn't want to have me taken away from her and given to some stranger, so she ran. She had been taking care of me all on her own since the day I was born," Justice explained.

"Wow! I had no idea," I responded honestly.

I would be lying if I said that her story didn't make me feel like a damn fool. I never knew that Val was a teen mom or that she grew up on the streets taking care of a newborn by herself. She looked way older than thirty- two when I had her killed. I would've thought that she was in her early fifties.

Drugs were a powerful thing. They had a way of aging a person to look twice their age.

"Even though I blame you for getting my mom hooked on drugs, the truth is that she was hooked long before you came around. My mom did what she had to do to support me, so sometimes she found herself doing things that would make other people's stomach turn. She was tricking at a young age and needed the drugs and alcohol to help her get through," Justice explained.

The information that she shamelessly shared with me blew my mind. Clueless to everything she revealed made me realize that I didn't know Val half as well as I thought.

After listening to her story, I wished I had heard it before I did away with her mom. Not to say it would have made a difference or not, but I probably would have looked at her in another light.

Maybe as a mom doing what she had to do to take care of her child instead of a dope fiend in search of her next fix. Another tear slipped from Justice's eye, and I pulled her close to me.

"Come here," I urged.

When she came closer, I gently wrapped my arms around her as she snuggled into my chest. Close to me, I held her and let her cry for as long as she wanted to.

As badly as I craved Justice's body before, dick wasn't what she needed to make her feel better. What my wife needed in this moment was a man who would show her empathy and compassion.

That was the man who I planned on being. It was only right since I was the one responsible for her pain.

"You okay, baby?" I asked several minutes later when she finally calmed down.

"I'm sorry if I ruined the night," she mumbled through her sobs.

"Not at all. We had a great night, and I'm happy you feel comfortable enough with me to talk about your mom. I didn't know any of the stuff you told me. I wish Val had shared some of that shit with me. It would've helped me to understand her better," I admitted.

"My mom had always been a very shy person. She didn't share things with anybody but me," Justice revealed. "I haven't even shared any of this with Rachel and she's my closest friend."

"Really? Why haven't you spoken to her about it?"

"Even though she's my best friend, there has always been pity in her eyes for me. I couldn't tell her all that me and my mom have been through. I didn't want to see any more of those pitiful expressions on her face. You don't pity me, so..." She shrugged her shoulders as she rested her head back against my chest.

"Well, I'm glad I'm here for you," I whispered as I kissed her forehead.

"Yea, I'm glad too. I literally have no family left now that my mom is gone," she admitted as she began to cry again. I stroked her shoulder gently as I held her.

"That's not true. You have me. I'm your husband now, so that makes me family," I stated.

"You're right."

"And you have my grandmother too..."

My last comment caused Justice to bust out laughing, which I was happy about because it helped to lighten the mood between us. "No, you didn't bring your grandmother into this after what happened with her earlier," she said as she laughed harder.

Well, I was glad she wasn't crying anymore, so I started laughing as well.

"I don't mean to laugh at your grandmother. It's just the way her wig looked when she came out the house!" Justice continued to crack up with laughter. "It was all tilted to one side. I mean, her side part was all the way on her right ear, and then she kept trying to blow her hair out of her eyes!" She started mimicking my grandmother which only made us laugh harder than before.

That was just what we needed to switch the mood up. Not that I was looking to get all lovey dovey and shit, but I didn't like seeing my wife sad. It took a long time for us to get to the point where we were now.

When Justice first came to live with me, I couldn't even get her to look me in the eyes, much less have a genuine conversation with me about anything. Now, she was not only sharing her past experiences about her mom and upbringing, but she was in my bed doing it with lingerie on. Sexy like a muthafucka.

Wow, I really cared about Justice, more than I ever thought possible. The deeper I fell for her, the more I wondered if I was making things more crucial for myself and for her. What if she found out that I had something to do with Val's death?

What would she think about me then? Would she even care why I did it what I did? Would it matter? Probably not because I swear if someone killed my granny, I wouldn't give a fuck why they did it. Just the fact that they did it would have me ready to paint the whole town red with their blood.

That was exactly why I prayed every day that Justice never found out. Every single day...

Chapter Twelve

Justice Patterson

Even though I still didn't fully trust Quinton, he had given me the most amazing birthday. However, I still had my mom on my mind throughout the day. I would have been a fool if I didn't because this was the first birthday that I had to celebrate without her.

Although she hadn't always given me a gift, when she did give me one, it was always something bought from the corner store... a bag of my favorite chips, a pack of my favorite bubble gum or a pack of Ramen noodles. Early on in life I learned that it wasn't the gift that was given to you, it was the thought behind it.

All the gifts that Quinton showered me with today made me feel special, but truthfully, I would've been happy if he had given me a bag of Cheetos. Like I said, it wasn't the gifts or how much money he spent on them. It was the thought that he put behind the gifts.

And he definitely put a lot of thought into shopping for my gifts to make me feel special. I truly appreciated him for that. And the way he held me when I cried and stroked my shoulder... it had me feeling all warm and fuzzy. It felt so good to be in his arms, but I still found myself crying when I wanted to stop.

Thank goodness Quinton was a quick thinker and brought his grandmother up. That immediately took my mind off my sad thoughts. Yep, he knew just what he was doing because it worked.

Had me laughing my ass off knowing that the first thing that would pop into my mind was that wig that his grandma had on. The way her shit was all lopsided when she rushed out of the house was hilarious.

That really helped to lighten the mood for us. Lying there stroking his smooth chest made me feel good about where things were headed. Though I was still nervous about the two of us having sex because I had never done it before, I was game if he made the first move. I sure wasn't going to.

If Quinton wanted any of this, he would have to initiate it. Hopefully, he did. When though? I had no clue.

"You alright, baby?" he checked as he held me close and massaged my back which made me relax a bit more in his arms.

As Quinton leaned his head for a kiss, I thought it was going to be a simple peck like we had shared before, but it definitely was not that. It was much, much more.

The way he stuffed his tongue deep into my mouth forced me to open mine so that I could hungrily receive it. As we continued to kiss, our feelings became more passionate. Then Quinton pulled back and said, "I want you, but I don't wanna force you to do anything you aren't ready for."

"I'm ready, but I'm nervous."

"I get that. It's your first time being intimate. If you want me to stop, just let me know."

"I don't. I wanna try..."

To prevent me from saying something stupid, I quickly pulled him in for another kiss. This time, his mouth traveled from my lips to my neck to my breasts. The tingling sensation that flowed through me heightened my arousal and caused me to release a slight moan.

Just as my body relaxed, Quinton pulled the straps of my negligee off my right shoulder. Suddenly, I began to tremble with nervousness. The only thing that was holding me back were his lips all over me. They were making me feel as if I was powerless to stop it.

"Shit," I gasped loudly as he took my right breast in his mouth and circled my nipple with his tongue. That caused a feeling down below that I had never felt before.

The entire time he sucked both of my breasts, I wanted to fondle his stiff dick that was steadily poking me, but I couldn't bring myself to do it at first. When I did get up enough nerve, Quinton switched positions.

As he climbed on top of me and lowered his face near my private part, he kissed my belly and then the top of my lace panty. Using his tongue, he licked my coochie through the thin material. The anticipation of what was coming next made me shudder beneath him as he pulled my panty to the side.

Soon as his tongue actually touched my fleshy center, I nearly jumped out of my skin and the bed. It took everything in me to stay in place.

"You taste so fucking sweet, baby," Quinton whispered as he used his fingers to part my moistened crevice.

This gave his tongue easier access to circle inside me. It also gave me some shit I wasn't expecting. A fucking orgasm the second his mouth latched onto my clit.

"Oh shit!" I hissed as I tried to push his head out from between my legs.

It wasn't that I wanted him to stop because that shit was incredible, in a weird way. Maybe because I had never had anyone do that to me before. I never knew that I could feel this good. Like damn! I couldn't believe his tongue was actually inside my vagina! He was licking and sucking on my coochie like it was a popsicle on a hot day.

"Sssssss!" I hissed as my body shook savagely. I had no idea what was happening to me. It was like I had no control over the way I was reacting. "Oh my God! Oh my God!" I cried.

Quinton continued to lick and suck on my vagina for several more minutes making the same explosion go off between my thighs. When he finally came up for air, his face was all wet. Once he wiped the moisture off using the back of his hand, he hovered over me and brought his lips to mine again.

Our tongues danced in each other's mouths as he removed my panty. After he slipped off his pajama bottoms next, he paused and asked, "Are you sure this is what you want?"

"Uh huh," I mumbled because I was feeling a type of way that was hard to describe. I couldn't even trust myself to speak.

As Quinton brushed his penis against my vagina, I became a jumble of nerves. My body shivered and quivered as he inserted himself inside me.

"Oh sssssshiiit!" I hissed.

The pressure that I felt down there as I tried to accept what he had to offer was indescribable. As I widened my legs, he pushed a bit further inside me and I did my best to receive him.

In and out, Quinton pumped slowly as my vagina tried to adjust to his girth. I wasn't sure how I was supposed to feel, but it was a bit painful.

"Relax babe. It'll feel better in a bit," he assured.

I tried to trust that he knew what he was talking about, so I did my best to relax. After a few minutes, I realized that he was right. The more I relaxed, the better it felt. That put me at ease to enjoy sex more.

And boy, did I enjoy it!

By the time we were done, I was breathing heavily but very satisfied. "How are you feeling, baby? You good?" Quinton asked in one breath.

"Amazing and I'm great!" I expressed as I placed my hand over my heart and felt the rapid pounding.

"I definitely enjoyed making love to my wife," he confessed happily as he held me close.

Our bodies were sweaty even though the air conditioner was blowing full blast. To get more comfortable, I partially pulled the sheet over me and thought about what had just happened.

Damn, I couldn't believe I had just had sex for the first time. Even more so, I couldn't believe it was with my husband. Quinton Marshall of all people. Never in my wildest dreams did I think that was going to happen.

Never did I even consider to connect with Quinton on a level this deep. While I was supposed to be keeping my walls up, there I was laying here allowing him to enter them. Why?

Why had I allowed him to sex me down like that? What in the hell was I thinking? Better question... why did I marry this man when I knew he was hiding shit from me about my mother's death?

Who was I kidding? I knew exactly why I let him get close to me. How could I not when he was so damn handsome and sexy as fuck? Not to mention, he had also been treating me like a queen. He had been taking care of me in ways I had never been taken care of before. It made me want to be honest and vulnerable with him. I just wasn't sure that was such a good idea. Damn, I sure needed someone to talk to about all this. I needed Rachel. I couldn't wait to tell her that I finally did it!

Considering how upset she was when she found out I was married, I didn't know how she would take that news. Hell, maybe that was something I should keep to myself. I mean, I didn't want her to feel like I was bragging or anything because she didn't even have a man right now.

Rachel used to tell me about this guy she was dating, but never told me his name or anything about him. Come to think of it, I wasn't sure if they were still seeing each other. If they were, she sure hadn't mentioned the last time we talked. That was quite a while ago.

Since I had been so busy stepping into my new role as Quinton's wife, I barely had time for myself. Plus, now that I had finally consummated my marriage by performing my wifely duty, I was sure I would be even more occupied than before.

Lord, help me because I was not ready!

Chapter Thirteen

Shawn Fulcher
The following week...

After Rachel pulled that knife on me and cut my face, I went to the hospital, got stitches then went back to get my shit out of the room. There was no way that I was staying in that same hotel suite without killing that bitch, so I checked into a nicer spot up the street.

Thankfully, we were able to handle all of our business, but when it was time to leave, I left Rachel's ass right back in San Antonio. Shit, she had enough dough to hop a flight back or rent a vehicle and drive home all on her own. She was no longer any of my concern.

When I made it back to Houston, I knew Quinton would have to be the first person I saw. He was going to have to figure out something else because that chick wasn't about to be anywhere around me. Not after slicing me in my face like that. The doctor told me that I was going to have a lifelong scar behind that shit. Ugh, I wanted to kill that fucking bitch!

"Here this bitch go now," I scoffed as I saw Rachel's name pop up on my screen while my cell continued to buzz.

The only reason why I decided to pick up was because I knew she was probably wondering where I was. Oh, fucking well!

"What?" I answered.

"Where are you?" she inquired.

"What you mean?"

"I mean, I'm over here at the hotel waiting for you to come get me. So, I'll ask again, where are you?" she asked. "I'm getting tired waiting out here for you!"

"Shit, you gon be waiting a long ass time if you waiting on me to come and get you," I said with a chuckle.

"What you mean by that?" she asked.

"What the fuck you think I mean?"

"I don't know. Why don't you just tell me?"

"I'm almost back in Houston!" I informed her. "So, you need to find your own way back."

"Wow! Are you serious right now?!" she asked, and I could hear the anger in her voice.

"Dead ass!"

"Are you really that petty to leave me all the way out here like that, Shawn? Are you that mad?"

"That you cut my fuckin' face?!" I checked because what the hell she thought? Did she think I was happy about that shit? That chick was lucky she was still breathing.

"What did you expect, Shawn?" she countered.

"Well, what did you expect, Rachel? That I was gonna let you ride three hours in the car with me after that shit! You must be fucking crazy." I laughed.

"So, I guess I gotta Uber..."

"Do whatever the hell you gotta do. You claim to be a grown fucking woman, so get off my line and figure that shit out!"

After I hung up on her, I blocked her ass. There was no need for that bitch to call my phone ever again.

To take my mind off things, I shot Syanna a text and told her that I made it home. Since Doreen didn't know I came back early, I could kick it with Syanna in peace.

"Cool," I chanted as Syanna hit me back and said she would be over after her photoshoot.

Just as quick as a smile spread across my face, a frown was soon to follow. It was always some bullshit.

"Shit, now, here she go!" I complained.

It was Doreen was calling me again. She was about to drive me crazy about a chick that I hadn't even fucked.

"What?" I repeated when I connected my baby mama's call.

"That's the way you answer the phone when you know it's me calling!"

"What do you want, Doreen? I'm tired and I need to sleep before I hit the road back to H-Town." I lied.

"So, you ain't got time to talk to yo baby mama?" she asked with a nasty attitude. "I know you wanna see Laya soon as you get back."

Sure, I wanted to see my daughter, but I couldn't do it right now. Not when Doreen thought I was still in San Antonio.

"I'll see y'all sometime tomorrow. I'll probably stop by there and bring y'all some food or something," I offered.

Obviously, that wasn't good enough for Doreen because she started cussing me out and calling me a deadbeat daddy. As tired as I was, I didn't even care. I just wanted to nap for a few hours.

For that to happen, I left my cell in the living room and went to bed. Only I didn't get the opportunity to shut my eyes after I cut off the lights because of the sound of the front door slamming.

After I jumped up, I grabbed my gun out of the drawer, took the safety off, and cocked it. I ran out into the living room ready to take aim until I saw my brother Square. What the hell did I tell him about using his key to just walk into my place without a warning? Then he had the nerve to bring his girl, Frankie with him.

I already knew I was screwed because she would surely tell Doreen that I was back in town. She couldn't hold water, so I knew damn well she wouldn't be able to hold on to this little tidbit of information.

"Nigga! That's how the fuck they make angels!" I hissed as I lowered my heater and shook my head.

"I'm sorry, bro. Shit, I didn't know you were here! I thought you weren't coming back until tomorrow. I was just stopping by to pick up the liquor I left over here the other night," Square explained as I thought about how Doreen found out where I was and who I was with.

"Wait, by any chance, did you tell Frankie about me going to San Antonio?"

"Was it a secret?" he questioned and shrugged his shoulders.

"No, but why would you tell her that Rachel was with me when you knew it was a business trip?" I asked. "Knowing how big her mouth is!"

"For one, don't be talking about me like I'm not standing right here!" Frankie complained as she rolled her eyes while adding a dramatic neck roll. "And two, you know Square tells me everything, so if Doreen asks me, I'm gonna tell her..."

"And Square, you too dumb to know that shit!" I shot towards him.

From the way the nigga shook his head, he didn't give a damn that he was bringing more drama in my life. That was messed up because it seemed as if Frankie had Doreen's back more than my brother had mine.

"Whatever nigga. I'm about to get my shit and get on outta here! Ain't nobody trying to be in that shit you got going on with Doreen."

"Wouldn't be no shit with Doreen if you and yo girl would keep my business to y'all fuckin' selves!"

When Square turned on the big light, him, and Frankie both looked at me and gasped. I almost forgot that I had stitches on my cheek until my brother began to question me.

"What the fuck happened to you?"

As I stood there and debated on whether to tell him the truth or not, especially in front of Frankie's messy ass, there was a loud banging on the door. Before I could make a move to go and see who it was, Doreen was storming in.

"You just walking up in here like this is your place and shit! You got a key too?!" I questioned angrily.

"What? No!" she yelled.

"How the fuck you just walk up in here then?"

"The door was unlocked fool!"

The first person I looked at was Frankie. "You left the door open for her, huh?"

"Ah, huh?"

When Frankie struggled to answer me, I knew what they were up to. I just prayed my brother wasn't in on it.

"What the hell do you want and where's Laya?" I asked.

"Don't worry about Laya!" Doreen replied. "I wanna know why you lied and said you were still out of town. How long have you really been back, Shawn?"

"You know what? It's funny how you have all the time in the world to come see me and will do whatever you have to in order to make it happen. Oh, but you won't do that same shit for me to see my daughter. See, that right there is that bullshit."

"Ask him where that cut on his face came from," Frankie instigated, which made me want to put her out. "Me and Square been tryna figure it out since we got here."

When Doreen came closer, her mouth dropped. "You got stitches? What the hell happened to you, Shawn?" she questioned sounding concerned as she tried to inspect my face closer.

"Nothing. It ain't..."

"Look at this shit!" Frankie blurted out as she ran over to Doreen and shoved her cell in her face. "This bitch Rachel online bragging about cutting a nigga. Could she be talking about you, Shawn?"

If I could have run out of my own house to avoid what was coming next, I would have. Unfortunately, Doreen was blocking the front door.

"Nigga, why the fuck would she cut you?" she pressed as she walked up on me.

"Look, I'm warning you, D, baby mama or not, I'm not about to stand here and keep letting you disrespect me. Now, if I put you on your back for coming up in my face, I'm gonna be wrong. That's your problem now. Always wanna be the man of the relationship. That's why a nigga ain't fucking with you now..."

"I'm fucking tired of you disrespecting me, Shawn!"

"Bitch..."

POW!

Whatever that chick picked up and hit me with had me seeing nothing but stars before my body crashed to the floor. Then there was darkness...

"Shawn! Shawn! Are you okay?" Square yelled as I tried to pry my eyes open.

As I felt the back of my head pounding like crazy, I quickly scanned the room and saw that we were now there alone. "What happened? Where that bitch go?"

"Nigga, you got knocked the fuck out!" Square mocked the dude from the movie, *Friday*. "Her and Frankie ran up outta here before you woke up and tried to shoot at them."

Now, I was mad enough to go after Doreen. That chick had seriously lost her damn marbles. What the hell was going on with those females?

First, Rachel sliced me and now this! Man, I had to find me a real one and quit fucking with those lunatics.

"No, seriously, bro. You okay?" Square repeated as he helped me off the floor.

Just as I got to my feet, my door swung back open. Without thinking first, I snatched my gun off the floor beside me and aimed it that way.

"Wait! It's me, Shawn! Syanna! You told me to come over!"

Hell, with all the commotion, I had forgotten all about shooting her that text. Damn!

"Sorry about that shit," I apologized and lowered my weapon once again.

"It's okay, but are you alright? What happened to your face and why are you holding the back of your head? Did someone try to rob y'all?" Syanna probed.

Instead of telling her the truth or making a story up, I let her run with hers. It was much simpler.

"Go wait in my room, baby," I instructed with a smack on her ass. "I'm gonna walk my brother out. I'll be in there in a few minutes."

"Okay." Syanna giggled and did as she was told.

When she was out of earshot, I told Square to make sure Frankie didn't know that I had company. "Nigga, I'm serious. This one time, can you please do as I ask? Please."

"After what I just saw, I totally understand. Someone could've gotten killed tonight and I wouldn't want to see that happen, especially if it were you, bro."

Maybe now that nigga got it. After all the times I reminded him not to speak my business to anybody, this dude constantly pillow talked with his girl. And Frankie was nothing but a messy ass bitch!

No matter what my brother told me, I had never spoke his business to anybody, especially not to Doreen's ass! Square knew just as well as I did about how close Frankie was to my baby mama. He should have never spoken my business to his girl.

Hell, he was worse than some of these messy bitches in the hood.

That nigga just couldn't keep his lips tight. How hard was that to do?

Sheesh!

Chapter Fourteen

Doreen Collins

"Did this nigga really try to play me?" I panted as Frankie, and I made it back to our apartment. "And were you really about to stay there with Square and Quinton and let me leave alone after everything that had just happened? That wasn't cool, boo."

"I'm here with you, ain't I?" Frankie complained and cut her eyes. "I'm not gonna keep doing that shit with you though, Doreen. I done told you more than once. I'm not gonna keep having your back on some dumb shit when it's gonna keep me and that nigga, Square arguing. We have a peaceful relationship and I want it to stay that way."

"So, let me get this straight, Frankie. While Shawn's constantly making me miserable, you're worried about how it's gonna affect you and Square's relationship! Is that what you're telling me?"

"Why wouldn't I worry? You and Shawn had a toxic relationship, and y'all need stay broken up. Continuing to be with him for the sake of your child isn't a good reason for y'all to be together, and I don't wanna lose my man like you lost yours..."

"Bitch, I love you, but right now the shit you're saying is about to get you punched in your mouth!"

"You know what? Because I love you, I'ma let you have this shit! You're obviously miserable and misery loves company..." With that, she turned her back and walked away.

Frankie knew that she didn't want any of these paws on her, so she did the smart thing. She went to her bedroom and closed herself in.

After she left me to myself, I went to get my cell then sat down on the sofa in the living room. My first notion was to hit Rachel up on social media but since she had me blocked, I couldn't use the app on my phone. Instead, I had to get on the desktop that we had in the dining room. That was where Frankie stayed logged in which made it easy for me to open up her page to get at Rachel using her profile.

What I was about to do may have been disrespectful, but in my mind, it was necessary.

"Here she go right here," I whispered to myself as I clicked on Rachel's page and jumped into her inbox to tell her who I was and why I was calling.

Me: Hey Rachel, it's Doreen. I need to talk to you so hit me back when you get a chance so we can have that conversation

Several minutes later, she finally decided to reply to my messages which meant that I had her attention.

Rachel: Girl bye! Using someone else's profile to contact me. Whatever you need to address is not

that serious! Go play in traffic or something but get the hell out my DM!

Oh, now this bitch had me hot! She had no idea who she was playing with or the hell that I was about to put her through!

Forget all the messaging. That took up too much time and energy that I didn't have, so I decided to call her through the app.

Unfortunately, that shit ended up being a total bust because Rachel wasn't saying anything that I wanted to hear. All she wanted to do was talk shit about me using someone else's profile to hop in her inbox uninvited. She said that I was harassing her then told me to leave her alone. *Ain't that some shit?*

What was she going to do if I didn't? Not a damn thing, so she was wasting her bad breath and my valuable time.

"Well, if you don't wanna tell me if you're fucking my baby daddy or not, tell me this... why the hell you cut his face up then?"

"Why the hell you calling me to ask that shit? Why not ask him? I mean, you obviously saw the stitches and shit, so why not just ask him why instead of calling me with this bullshit?"

"I did see his face, but he didn't tell me why you did it! That's why I'm asking you... woman to woman," I told her again. "Just keep it a hundred!"

"Woman to woman!" she stated as she laughed. "I hate when women say *woman to woman* when they wanna know something, but soon as you tell them what they're asking, the woman becomes a bitch and ho' and all that other shit! You are there with your baby daddy, ask him what happened to his face!"

Man, this bitch had me wanting to fuck her up! If I ever saw this heifer in person again, I would swing at her on sight just for coming at me like that. I just asked that ho' a simple fucking question! Why was it so hard for Rachel to answer it?

"Stop playing fucking games and just tell me what I wanna know! If you won't do it for me, do it for yourself," I suggested.

"For myself?" she asked with a chuckle.

"Yes, for yourself, so I won't have to come for you, bitch!"

"Who you need to go after is your fresh ass baby daddy!"

"My baby daddy was injured cuz of your ass!"

"Yea, but if he hadn't come into my hotel room and tried to rape me..."

When Rachel said what she said, I almost busted out laughing. Why would Shawn have to try and take the neighborhood slut's pussy when he could get it from anywhere or anybody else who was willing to give it? Shit, Rachel wasn't that cute and she damn sure wasn't special. She had to be kidding.

"Bitch please! Why the hell would Shawn need to try and rape you? You really will say anything you can to keep me from beating yo ass..."

"Girl ain't nobody worried about you!" Rachel scoffed. "You may be big and bad, but bitch as the saying goes, the bigger they are the harder they fall. You gonna find that shit out if you keep coming for me, Doreen. Fuck around and get taken down to your knees. You better pay attention and tread lightly," she threatened boldly. "You ain't the only bitch who knows how to fight! Try me if you want to."

Rachel must've had one too many cups of courage to talk to me like that. How dare she!

Ugh, on sight, it was on! Just because I didn't know where she lived, didn't mean I couldn't get to her.

By the way our streets talked, finding out where she rested her head wouldn't be hard to do.

"Stay away from me and tell yo homegirl, Frankie, I'm blocking her ass too! Y'all bitches need to find a job or a hobby or something! You obviously got too much time on your fucking hands bitch! And wait until I talk to Shawn..."

"Why you wanna talk to Shawn?" I pressed before she hung up on me and did just what she said she would do. She blocked Frankie's page too.

As I sat up in the chair and spun from the desktop, I heard Frankie running down the hallway like somebody was chasing her. Basic instinct placed me on high alert.

"Seriously, Doreen?" Frankie dashed in the dining room screaming and hollering.

"What?"

"Were you using my page to cuss Rachel out? Oh, and before you sit there and lie to my face, know that I have all the messages on my phone. It's all connected."

Busted! But I didn't give a damn. That was what friends were for. If a bitch threatened me, she threatened Frankie too!

"So what? What's the big deal? You come running in here like I stole your credit card and charged it up or something! Damn, Frankie! It ain't even that serious. I only used your inbox call feature to get at her stupid ass!"

"Why? Shawn said he wasn't messing with her and after I saw his face, I believe him. You should too, instead of always trying to fight everybody. That shit don't change nothing. After it's over, you're still mad. Win or lose!"

Was Frankie still trying to clown me about Ashleigh getting the best of me? I prayed not because the way I was feeling, she would want to back off me.

"You know what, Frankie? I didn't ask for your advice, but I'll give you some..."

"Oh, shit! Here we go with the bullshit."

"You sure are feeling yourself."

"What do you mean by that, Doreen?" she asked.

"I mean, every time we agree to disagree, you have to take a shot about me losing that fight," I stated but Frankie brushed off what I said and got back to the advice I offered. Smart ass.

"Whatever, Doreen. I'm not tryna hear that stuff. All I wanna know is what advice could you possibly have for me?" Frankie blurted out, interrupting me once again.

"Do us both a favor and don't tell me shit about Shawn... no, I take that back. Tell yo nigga to stop pillow talking and telling folks business..."

"You fucking pressed me to tell you where yo baby daddy was and who he was with! What I look like not telling you? We're supposed to be best friends. And I still went against my man knowing how he felt about that shit! I'm not gonna keep doing that shit. I love Square and if you loved Shawn like you said you did, you would back up and give him the space you asked him for! That's what started this mess in the first place!"

Fuck what Frankie was saying. Acting like her and Square had the perfect little relationship. Shit, that nigga cheated more than his brother and she knew it.

"For real, Frankie. Lately it ain't been feeling like we're tight like we used to be." I sighed and cut my eyes.

"It's just that I'm tired of seeing you act a fool behind Shawn when he ain't thinking about you..."

WHAP!

Shit, I didn't mean to slap Frankie, but the harsh truth that she spat stung hard enough to force tears from my eyes.

"Bitch really!" she howled.

I wanted to say sorry, but I didn't think that would matter to Frankie one bit. At least not right now because before I could move or apologize, she charged at me.

That shock lasted all of three seconds then I realized that Frankie was actually fighting me. I mean seriously hitting and punching me! The last thing I wanted to do was fight with my best friend, but I'd be damn if I would let her punk me! She was swinging on me, and I was swinging on her until I got enough of her shit!

"Get the fuck off me Frankie!" I hissed and swung her onto the sofa.

When her body bounced from the cushions to the floor, it created a loud thud, and she started hollering. Damn!

"I'm sorry, Frankie!" I apologized and tried to help her up.

"Don't fucking touch me!" she cried and struggled to get on my feet. "After all these years and all that we've been through... you wanna put yo hands on me because I told you the truth, D?"

"I'm sorry. I'm really sorry!" I cried.

I never meant to hurt my friend, but she just said some shit I didn't want to hear. She was right that we had been through a lot over the years. I never expected to get into an actual fist fight with my bestie, but she had pushed me to the limit, and I just couldn't hold back any longer.

Never did I intend for us to physically attack one another. Never...

"Fuck you! Fuck you and fuck Shawn! Y'all fucking deserve each other!"

Frankie didn't want to hear my apology. She was too upset right now, and I could understand that.

Without absolutely no eye contact, she got up from the floor and limped to her room then slammed the door behind her. Now I felt terrible, and I didn't even want to be here while she was that mad.

"Fuck it!" I shrugged and packed a small bag to go to my mom's house.

Since I had to pick Laya up in the morning anyway, it wasn't a big deal. The only thing I could think about was that slap I dealt to Frankie.

Instead of taking my anger out on my best friend, I should've been taking it out on Shawn and that bitch Rachel. Oh, and if I caught Syanna back up in the mix, she would get it too.

"Why?" I sighed as I used the drive to my mother's house to think.

To create total silence, I cut of the satellite radio so that I could go over everything that had been happening in my life. Where did things go wrong?

When Shawn came to mind first, I thought about how I had been acting. It didn't take long for me to realize that it really may have been my fault that things were so bad between us. Why? Because like Frankie said, I was the one who requested the break between us.

If I had any idea that it would backfire on me like this, I would've never suggested it. I only did it because I thought it would make him miss me enough to want to act right. Oh, how wrong I was!

"Ugh!" I grunted out in frustration as I arrived at my mother's.

Once I parked and killed the engine, I grabbed my bag off the back seat and went inside without thinking about what my mother was going to say. With me showing up out of the blue when she wasn't expecting me until the morning was sure to set her off.

Knowing my mom, she was going to add her two cents to my business and make me more irritated than I was before. Maybe I should have rented a room instead of coming here.

"Why are you here with a bag?" she asked soon as I crossed the threshold.

"Me and Frankie got into it," I briefly explained, hoping she would leave it at that.

"What you mean got into it?"

A very concerned expression appeared on my mother's face as she took a seat at the counter. She then looked up at me and told me to sit.

"Where's Laya?" I inquired in attempt to change the subject.

"Faye came by with Vanity and Amelia to see if Laya could play with them. So, they're playing next door. I was planning to go get her in a few minutes," she said. "But sit here and let me talk to you."

"Mom, before you start preaching..."

"Before I start preaching nothing, you sit here and tell me why you got into a fight with your best friend. Why, Doreen?"

"I didn't tell you we got into a fight. I told you that we got into it..."

"You got scratches on your face Doreen! It doesn't take a genius to figure out that the two of you were fighting. And now, I need you to tell me why. Why were you fighting your best friend?"

"Because she was being disrespectful."

"In what way?"

"Just take my word for it... she was disrespectful to me," I replied with a smirk.

"I need you to tell me how because you've been friends with Frankie for a long time, and the two of you have never been in a physical altercation. What made this time different?"

"Ma, she just pissed me off, okay?"

"No, it's not okay. Now you're either gonna tell me what happened or I'm gonna get on the phone and call Frankie and ask her myself."

"Wow! It ain't even that serious," I said as I blew out an exasperated breath.

"She was talking shit about me and Shawn..."

"You and Shawn!" she expressed as she rolled her eyes. "Let me tell you something... if you out here fighting your best friend behind that no- good dog, I oughta whip your ass myself, Doreen! Frankie has been there for you through thick and thin! She was there for you when your daddy died! She was there for you when you had Laya! And she was and has been there for you every single time Shawn made you cry! And you got the nerve to fight her behind his ass! That's your problem now, Doreen. You always gotta put your hands on somebody when you don't like what they say or do. Is that really your solution for everything? If you think it is, I feel sad for you because if you don't meet your match, or get killed trying to whoop everybody, you'll surely end up in jail. What's gonna happen to Laya then? I'm gonna have to fight a street runner like Shawn for temporary custody? Do you even think about things like that?"

"Ma, it wasn't even like that..."

"Then please enlighten me about what it's about," she urged as she eyed me up and down.

Now that my mother had me on the spot, I didn't know how to answer her. I didn't want to tell her everything, but if I didn't and she called Frankie, I knew she would rat me out.

Aware that I was wrong to fight with Frankie, I began to feel worse than I did before. All she had ever done to have my back, and I went and put my hands on her? That was dead ass wrong, and I never should have done that. Never...

As I sat there and looked into my mom's eyes as I relayed the story about what happened to her, I knew I had fucked up. Big time.

"So, let me get this right. You used Frankie's Facebook account to contact some girl that went out of town with Shawn and sliced his face. You and the female got into it on Frankie's account, and when she confronted you about it, you slapped her. Is that how that went down?"

"Pretty much," I said as I shrugged my shoulders.

"You were wrong! Dead wrong, and you owe her an apology," my mom fussed with a stern expression.

"I tried to apologize before I left, but she didn't wanna hear it."

"Then you need to give her a little time to cool off, but you for sure owe that girl an apology. You obviously have no idea what true friendship is. You truly have to know how to be a friend in order to have a friend. You don't turn your back on them when they've been there for you for years. Not behind a man who constantly dogs you out. If your dad ever treated me the way Shawn treats you, death wouldn't have taken him out, I would have. There would've been no second, third, or tenth chances because I value myself more than that and you need to do the same, Doreen."

"You trying to say I don't value myself?" I asked in awe.

"You don't know your worth Doreen, otherwise, you would never allow that man to treat you like he treats the bottom of his shoes. Just walking all over you and you stand for it. You think that because the two of you have a child together, you have to stay together? No, buddy!"

"Laya deserves to be raised by both parents..."

"Laya will still be raised by both of her parents. You and Shawn will always be her mom and dad. That is never going to change. What Laya needs are two parents who can raise her the right way. You can't be the best mom for her if you have no self-worth. Running around fighting different women behind a man is ridiculous. And now, you've gotten into a fist fight with YOUR BEST FRIEND!! You have to see how wrong that was!" she expressed as she shook her head from side to side. "I'm disappointed in you, sweetheart."

That shit sliced at my heart. This was the very first time that my mom ever voiced that she was disappointed in me. I never wanted her to ever feel that way about. That shit really had me in my feelings.

The unfamiliar pain struck me hard enough to cause tears to stream from my eyes. If my mother was that disappointed in me, Frankie was probably even more so. Dang, I hoped she was okay.

"I don't know what to do ma," I confessed with a sniffle. "Frankie is pissed, and she won't talk to me. I can't fix it if she won't accept my apology."

"Just give her a lil time. You mean as much to her as she means to you. I'm sure she did not expect you to put hands on her," my mom explained. "I sure she was just as surprised as I was to hear you did that crap."

"And I'm sorry for it," I repeated as I dried my tears using the sleeve of my shirt.

"It will be okay, Doreen," she assured. "Right now, I'm gonna go next door and get Laya from your Aunt Faye's. You wanna come?"

"No ma'am. I think I'm gonna go in the bathroom and wash my face before Laya comes in."

"Yea, and don't worry. You and Frankie will make up before you know it," she promised as she hugged me tight.

"I hope you're right," I replied with a hopeful grin.

"Mama is always right." She teased with a warm smile before walking out the front door.

While she went to get Laya, I went to wash my face. After I cut the water on, I glanced up into the mirror and gasped loudly. All the scratches from the fight shocked me. They were on my cheeks, forehead, and chin.

Just the sight of them made me feel like crying all over again. I still couldn't believe that I got into it with my best friend.

As much as I loved Frankie, we just had to find a way to make up. Without her, I would be lonely and lost. She was more like a sister to me than a friend and I didn't know what I'd do if she didn't forgive me.

She just had to...

Chapter Fifteen

Rachel Gwinn

As if I didn't have enough issues of my own, now Shawn's crazy ass baby mama wanted to add me to their pot of problems. That bitch had the nerve to call me from Frankie's account to argue about why I cut her man's face. She needed to ask his ass that, not me! And if he didn't want to tell her, then that was on her!

Quinton knew exactly what he was doing when he sent me and Shawn to San Antonio together. Then to get us one room when he knew the hotel was fully booked. That shit was either a setup, or a test. Either way, it didn't work.

There was no way on God's green earth that I would cross that line with Shawn. That was what no one seemed to understand, especially Doreen who was calling me any way that she possibly could. Just desperate as could be.

Normally, I wouldn't argue with her when I knew that she was a certified nut, but I had enough of her and that foul ass mouth of hers. If she was smart... never mind, that bitch couldn't be if she was still trying to engage in street fights behind that no-good baby daddy of hers. Didn't nobody have time for that shit anymore. We weren't teenagers anymore. Like, grow the hell up! Especially Shawn's childish ass.

That dirty dog had the nerve to leave me here in San Antonio while he took his ass back to Houston! What kind of sense did that make? Regardless of what happened in that room, he brought me here, so he should've provided me with a ride back. If was that big of a deal and he didn't want to be all up in my face like he had been, I would have gladly ridden in the back seat. He didn't have to leave me!

That was some bullshit and I damn sure called Quinton to tell him about his damn boy. It took for the voicemail to come on after the first ring to remind me that I was still blocked.

Damn that Quinton for putting me off on Shawn while he ignored me and went to slept with my friend. He could deny that shit for however long he wanted to, but I knew he had done it.

Married or not, I couldn't give Quinton up because I had become attached to that man. Too damn attached.

Only if I would have told Justice about me and Quinton before she ran off with him. At least if I had shared my relationship with him to her, she would have known not to marry his ass. But she went in blindly and that was partly my fault.

It really made me felt bad that he hadn't told Justice about us or that I hadn't told her as soon as I found out they were married. But I promised myself that as soon as I got back to Houston, I was going to meet up with her and tell her everything. No matter how mad it would make Quinton.

Since I had already warned him that if he didn't tell Justice first, I would, it shouldn't come as a surprise to him. Unless he hadn't taken my threats seriously.

Knowing Quinton, he was still keeping Justice in the dark for his own personal reasons, but I was going to shed some light on everything once I got back. Something about this marriage reeked 'scandal' and I was going to find out what it was.

"Let me get up outta here," I spoke to myself as I packed the rest of my things.

While I was sitting there worried about everything else, I should've been focused on getting back to Houston. There was no way I could get an Uber to take me all the way back, so I was going to have to try and catch an expensive last minute flight or get a rental from the airport.

It didn't take long to decide once I arrived at the airport only to discover that there weren't any available flights until late that night. Since I wasn't waiting that long, a rental car was my only other option.

Before I went up to the Avis counter, I sat down and looked up their policy. When I saw that I had to be twenty- one, I silently thanked Quinton for the driver's license that he duplicated with all my actual information on it. The only thing that was changed was my birthdate.

Fuck what Shawn said about Quinton doing this shit for everyone. I was just glad that he did it for me. It certainly was about to come in handy right now.

With my fake license in hand, I went up to the counter and was greeted by a young Hispanic woman who smiled and greeted, "Hi, can I help you?"

"Yes ma'am. I need a car to get back to Houston. I got stranded her with no way home, so I'm praying that you can help me."

"Have you ever rented a car with us before?"

"No ma'am."

"I need your driver's license and a debit or credit card," she explained.

After I reached in my small purse, I pulled out the necessary information. Thank goodness that I had just opened a bank account about a month ago, because I didn't have any credit card. Instead, I handed her my debit card along with my driver's license.

Once she checked the two, she handed me a clipboard with some paperwork to fill out. "Just fill this out and bring it back once you're done."

As I stood to the side, I quickly filled out the paperwork. It took me several minutes to complete it, and when I did, I stepped back over to her and handed her the clipboard.

While she typed some information into the computer, she politely asked me what size vehicle I wanted. Like I knew what size they came in.

"It doesn't matter. I just need to get back home," I answered.

"I have a Nissan Versa or a Chevy Cruz. They're both compact cars but they're really good on gas and mileage," the agent explained.

"That's fine with me."

After going over the rules with me, she had me sign some papers before walking me outside. She brought the clipboard with her and handed it to me.

"We need to do a thorough check of the car for damages. That way when you bring it back, we'll know if there are any new damages," she explained.

The two of us walked around the car and checked it out. The only thing that we discovered was a small scratch on the passenger side door. Other than that, no other visible damages.

To complete the transaction, I signed and initialed where necessary. Next, she handed me the keys.

"Make sure you fill the gas tank before you return the car otherwise, the price of gas will double if we have to refill it."

"Yes ma'am, and thank you," I said.

"You're welcome. Have a safe trip back."

"Thanks."

Before I left the lot in my little rental car, I put my home address into the maps app on my cell. Once I pressed start, I headed to the highway.

Originally, I was not planning to drive nearly four hours back to the Houston area by myself. With no one to talk to I turned on the satellite radio and listened to some Hip Hop to keep me alert.

Nearly every song they played, I knew the words to and was able to sing right along with them. Thankfully, that helped the time pass quickly and by six that evening, I was back in the city.

As exhausted as I was, I couldn't resist the urge to roll through the hood to see if I could spot Quinton anywhere. Since I could keep the car until tomorrow, I was about to get my money's worth out of it.

"Damn, where he at?" I whispered to myself as I hit block after block.

When I didn't see Quinton or any of his workers that I knew well enough to question, I took a chance and called Justice to find out if they were together. If they weren't together, that meant he had to be somewhere out in the streets. If they were together, I had to find a way to get them apart so I could speak to my friend in private.

"Hey, Justice," I greeted.

I didn't know what she was doing before she picked up the phone, but I knew what it sounded like when she answered. I immediately rolled my eyes and wondered whether I should hang up on her or not.

"Hello," she answered breathlessly as she laughed. "Wait Quinton! Wait! Someone's on the phone!"

"You picked up the phone... really bae!" he spoke in the background.

"Justice! Uhm hello!" I spoke making sure that she knew I was bothered.

"Rach... Rach... aw shit, Rachel!" she stuttered.

"Hang up that phone!" Q ordered in the background. I could tell that he was aggravated, but I didn't care. I had called to talk to my best friend, and I wasn't hanging up until I said what I had to say.

"Justice don't hang up. It's im..."

CLICK!

What the fuck! Did she just hang up on me? I looked at the phone and sure enough the screen was black. Why the hell would she hang up on me? I called her back, but no answer. I called again and got sent straight to voicemail. That shit really hurt because if I was calling for an emergency, I couldn't even count on my best friend.

As I rode around looking for someone who could give me information on where I could find Quinton or Justice, I realized I wasn't getting anywhere. All I was doing was burning the gas in this little stupid ass car!

Left with no other options at the moment, I headed back to my apartment with my feelings distorted, and my hopes dashed. If Quinton was somewhere fucking Justice, he was dead wrong for that. He knew she was my best friend, and he still had sex with her. Maybe it was time for me to find another best friend because obviously Justice was more into Q than she was into our friendship.

In desperate need to talk to someone, I thought about my mom. She was the only one who could help me right now.

Although I hadn't told her that Justice had gotten married yet, she knew that my friend had come back to town because her neighbor was more than happy to share that news. Ever since then she had been asking when Justice was going to come by and see her, but I couldn't answer that question because I had no idea.

The only way to find out was to talk to her and that was just what I planned on doing. Just as soon as I got ahold of her...

Chapter Sixteen

Quinton Marshall

That bitch Rachel was stomping on my last fucking nerve! All these calls to Justice every five minutes had to stop. We couldn't even get it in good without her phone ringing.

"I can't believe you even answered that, baby," I complained as I attempted to climb right back on her, but after I hung up on her little bug- a- boo ass friend, Justice wasn't having it. Now, she was upset.

"She don't want shit and you know that baby!" I tried to convince her.

"I think she was saying it was important, but I couldn't find that out because you hung up on her, Quinton. Why would you do that?" Justice whined and got up out of the bed with her phone in hand.

Not wanting to argue, I let her be while I thought of a way to stop her from calling Rachel back. After that threat she made to tell Justice about us before I could do it, was haunting me. I had to beat her to the punch.

"Baby!" I yelled out anxiously. "Baby, baby! Come here!"

Justice came running back in the room with a panicked expression on her face. "What's wrong now?"

"We forgot to buy the tickets to the Beyonce concert. They went on sale this morning. I thought you wanted to go?"

When I told her to get online and pick out any seats that she wanted, she couldn't get on her cell fast enough. Now that Justice was wearing a smile again, I was good.

"While you do that, I'm gonna go call Shawn and check in with him about his run," I briefly explained.

Once I got downstairs and went into the den, I dialed Rachel up to see where her head was at. I needed to know how much time I had to tell Justice before she went blabbing her fucking mouth.

"Oh, now you wanna call me! After you broke my heart again! I can't believe you Q! You slept with my best friend! You did, didn't you?!" Rachel cried.

"I did that shit just to fuck with you. You know I ain't slept with Justice..."

"Then why did you marry her, Q?"

"For business reasons. That's all you need to know, so keep that shit to yourself."

Right now, I was willing to tell Rachel whatever lie she needed to hear just as long as she stayed away from both me and Justice. I just wasn't willing to give into her demands. She was crazy for even coming at me like that.

"If you meet me at my house and make love to me like you used to, I won't tell her nothing. I promise, Q. I just miss you and need you so much," she pleaded.

That begging ass bitch was bold for that one. To tell me to give into her demands so she won't snitch on me! Naw, Rachel wasn't running shit but her mouth and if she wasn't careful, she wouldn't be able to run that muthafucka for too much longer.

"I ain't coming over there and I told you that shit already."

"The choice is yours," Rachel taunted.

"There's repercussions and consequences if you do that shit. You know how the game goes. You cross me and you just may get crossed out."

"Wow! Was that a threat, Q? Are you threatening me again?"

"Didn't you just threaten me?" I pressed as I began to get more upset by the second. "Talking about telling Justice some shit."

"You heard me and I'm not playing the fool no more, Q!"

The more shit Rachel talked, the more I thought about just paying her off, but when I brought it up to her, she laughed. I guess she thought that those little bills she made up in San Antonio put her stupid ass at baller status. Nope. She had a lot to learn and a lot more money to make to get on my level.

"You know what? Maybe I should just tell Justice anyhow, Q. It ain't like you wanna fuck with me anymore and besides, she's my best friend. I don't wanna keep hiding this shit from her. She don't deserve that from me or you."

"Well then, just give me time to tell her myself, Rachel."

"That's Justice calling on the other line now. I gotta go."

Before I could bark out another demand, that bitch hung up on me. Worse than that, she was on the phone with my wife.

As I tried my darndest to come up with another distraction, I went upstairs to find Justice. When I located her in the bedroom chatting with Rachel, I immediately became nervous.

"I'm on my way over there. I can't even talk with my husband all up in my face like this. You can just tell me whatever you have to say when I get there."

Soon as they hung up, I asked if she got the tickets. "Yea, but I ain't worried about those tickets right now. Rachel needs me!"

"Fuck Rachel!" I expressed as she looked over and gasped at me.

"Why do you hate her so much?"

"Did you get good seats?"

Instead of answering Justice's question, I shot one back at her. As the conversation abruptly shifted, she told me all about our seats then turned and walked into the bathroom.

Without saying another word, Justice cut the water on and stepped out of her clothes. While she showered quickly, I stood there talking about the concert, but she didn't engage in the chat.

"Since you're just standing there, can you please hand me a towel?" she asked as she held her hand out.

After drying off inside the clear glass enclosure, she came out wrapped in her bath towel. When she avoided eye contact while she got dressed, I knew something was up.

"Where are you going?"

"To Rachel's. She's been trying to tell me something for a while now, but every time we get on the phone, you disrupt our conversation. It has to be really important cuz she keeps reaching out to me about it. BUT, thanks to you, she hasn't been able to. That's why I need to go over there. I know once we get face to face, she can vent or at least say whatever it is that she has to say, without any interruptions."

"Can't you just go tomorrow?"

"Q, I've been putting this off too long. I need to see my best friend. I love being here with you, but me and Rachel need to have that good old-fashioned girl talk to catch up on things. I really miss her, and I know she misses me too. Hell, I ain't even been over to her mom's place since my mom's passing. Ms. Nancy is the closest thing I have to a mother right now and I wanna go see her too."

There was no debating with Justice. Her mind was made up.

"I'll be back tonight and if I decide to stay over, I'll call and let you know," Justice said.

"Stay out all night?" I gasped.

"Quinton... Rachel and I may wanna drink or something. I'm not gonna drive all the way back out here under the influence."

"Well, I ain't comfortable with you sleeping out like that. You're a married woman now, so if you drink too much, just give me a call and I'll go by there and pick you up. You ain't gotta stay over there."

"You are really tripping, Q. I don't know what the big deal is. I'm just going over to Rachel's and maybe to her mom's. Nowhere else, so stop worrying so much," Rachel urged.

Little did she know, it wasn't her spending the night over there that worried me. It was what that big mouth bitch was going to tell her while she was there.

Shit, what was I going to do? How could I stop this from happening? Should I just tell her myself right now?

As I stood there thinking of a way to come clean about me and Rachel's past, Justice was putting on her shoes and grabbing her keys.

"Wait, baby. I wanted to talk to you before you leave," I told her as I followed her down the stairs and into the foyer.

"Nope, whatever it is you have to say, Quinton, it can wait until I get back. You do that shit every time..."

"What?"

"Think of shit to stop me from spending time with Rachel. I don't know if you just don't like her or you want me all to yourself, but whatever it is, you two are gonna have to learn to get along!" She smiled as she leaned in and gave me a kiss.

When her lips touched mine, any type of excuse to make her stay went right out the window. Just like Justice went right out the door. Damn!

Panic came over me as I watched her pull off. There had to be something that I could do.

Now that racing over to Rachel's like she wanted me to in the first place wasn't an option, I decided to call her instead. At this point, I was ready and willing to negotiate.

As I raced back upstairs to get my cell, I thought about what I would say to her. Fortunately, it all came to me once I dialed her number.

"What's this shit?" I scoffed as I got Rachel's voicemail on the first ring.

The same thing happened for the next ten minutes. That was how long it took me to figure out that the bitch had actually blocked me.

My last choice was to race my ass over there and try to stop this little meeting that Rachel set up for her to snitch to my wife. If I couldn't do that, I didn't know what was going to happen.

"Ugh, I should've just killed that bitch!"

As I sat and marinated on this shit for a minute, I realized it was all my fault. I had done such a great job of keeping Justice and Rachel apart for the past few months and I didn't use the time to come clean. That was my opportunity to fess up to Justice and explain everything to her my way, but I didn't do that. Instead, I kept that shit to myself thinking that Rachel loved me way too much to betray me that way.

Man, was I wrong! If that bitch had any real love for me, she would have never even thought to go to Justice and tell her about us. She would have just accepted the fact that I had moved on.

"I should've just given her the dick!" I stressed.

Had I done that, none of this would be happening. To get Justice to come back, I called her to see if I could maybe stop this train wreck from going down, but she didn't answer. I couldn't believe Justice was ignoring my calls this way. She had never done that before.

As determined as she was, I figured that Justice was really beginning to feel the guilt that she said had been eating her up. She hated how she had abandoned her friend the past few months.

"Fuck that!" I fumed as I grabbed my keys and left the house.

Justice had about a twenty- five minute lead, but if I just sat here and waited for the hammer to drop, I was going to drive myself crazy. I had to do something.

Now becoming desperate, I unblocked Rachel on Facebook and tried to call her from the messenger app. Of course, that shit- starting chick didn't answer.

That fucking girl was determined to ruin my relationship with Justice just because I didn't want her anymore. That was some crazy shit! Why couldn't she just move the hell on? I wouldn't be mad if she found another nigga to fuck because then she would leave me and mine to live in peace. Was that too much to ask?

"Let me hurry up and get over there before the damage is done," I chanted with worry as I mashed the gas and exceeded the speed limit.

The entire ride, I wondered what else was she going to tell Justice. With my bad luck, probably everything.

And then some added bullshit...

Chapter Seventeen

Justice Patterson

Boy, was I enjoying my afternoon with my husband. As it turned out, I liked Quinton way more than I thought I did. He was just so sweet and charming, which was the total opposite of who I thought he was. When I first met him, I thought he was a total jerk! But now, after spending some time with him these past few months, I realized that I had misjudged him.

But what I did notice was how he tried to keep me from talking or seeing Rachel. He didn't do it in a deliberate way, but he did it subtly. Whenever I had asked him why he didn't like her, he always claimed that he had nothing against her. Something inside told me differently.

That was exactly why I needed to find out what was so important when Rachel reached out and said she needed to see me. I could tell by the sound of her voice that it was something serious.

Since I had been avoiding time with my best friend to get to know my husband, I felt like I was neglecting Rachel when she needed me most. It was bad enough that I disappeared after my mother was killed and she couldn't be there for me.

Rachel actually thought I was dead. How fucked up was that? That shit had to tear her up because it would have done the same to me if something happened to Ms. Nancy.

No more though. I was about to be here for my best friend. Fuck what anyone else said or did to keep us apart.

Like the dirty shit Quinton pulled when he hung the phone up in Rachel's face. That right there definitely made me feel some kind of way and caused me to look at him sideways. If he didn't have anything against her the way that he claimed, he sure had a funny way of showing it. The way he acted earlier let me know that there was definitely some tension between them.

Besides the way that Quinton was behaving behind Rachel, she had been acting rather weird lately too. Like that way that she got so livid when she found out that I had married Quinton. The expression on her face when she saw my rings was one of total shock and disbelief. It was almost like watching a scene from a horror movie when the woman figured out the man that she loved was the killer. Straight creepy.

Even if I tried, I couldn't make her understand why I did what I did that day I went over there because as soon as Quinton found out where I was, he came to get me.

At the time, I thought he was doing it because he wanted me all to himself, but now I was starting to wonder. What the hell was he up to?

As I drove to Rachel's apartment, my phone rang. I already knew it was Quinton even before I saw his name light up on the screen.

If I answered it, I knew he was going to try and get me to go back home, so I didn't. All he wanted to do was continue to keep me away from Rachel and I couldn't risk that. I had to find out what was going on with her while I had the chance.

"Here we go." I sighed as I pulled into the parking lot of her apartment complex almost an hour later.

Once I parked in the lot closest to her apartment and right next to her car, I exited the vehicle and headed to the door. Before I could knock, she pulled it back like she had been watching for me through the blinds. She clearly had been drinking and her hair was disheveled like she had been running a pitchfork through it all day. What the hell was going on with her?

I immediately became nervous. "What's going on? Are you okay?" I asked as I faced her.

Rachel paced the room like a caged animal while she puffed on a Vape. "I'm fine. Where's Quinton? Is he with you? Did he follow you?" she asked as she nervously peeked through her blinds.

"No, I came by myself. He didn't want me to come though," I admitted as I shook my head from side to side. "For some reason, he doesn't want me to hang with you like we used to."

"I'm not surprised!"

"Why? Rachel what's going on?"

"Justice, I tried to be a good friend to you..."

"What are you talking about? You've been a great friend to me! I feel as though I haven't been a good friend to you lately though, and I'm sorry about that. I never meant to ignore you or our friendship or anything like that," I sincerely apologized.

"I know that's not all your fault. I know that Q has been keeping you away from me..."

"Yea, you're right about that. He tried to stop me from coming over here tonight..."

"I knew he would!"

"How did you know? I mean, I know the two of you have known each other since before we got married, but were y'all ever involved?" I asked, hoping that her answer would be no.

At this point, I just wanted Rachel to put my mind at ease and tell me that I was overreacting, but I had this gut feeling in the pit of my stomach that was telling me I wasn't.

"I'm sorry! I should've told you about all of this that day you showed up here when you came back to town wearing that wedding ring!" she confessed through trembling lips.

"Told me what about what? And what does this have to do with Quinton?" I asked needing her to be more specific.

BANG! BANG! BANG! BANG!

"RACHEL! JUSTICE! OPEN THE DOOR!!" Quinton yelled from the outside.

Rachel rushed to the door and pulled it back. "HA! I knew you would find your way here!" she scoffed as he brushed by her.

Quinton looked nervous and panicked, all rolled in one great big emotion. "Justice let's go!" he demanded as he grabbed my hand and pulled me towards the door.

Rachel stood in front of the door with tears running from her eyes. "NO! YOU'RE NOT GOING ANYWHERE UNTIL YOU TELL HER THE TRUTH!!" Rachel hollered.

"Rachel, get the fuck out the way!" Quinton stated in an angry tone.

In turn, she shook her head from side to side. "Uh uh! I'm not budging until you tell Justice the truth!" she cried. "There's more to this story! Much more!"

My nerves became a jumbled mess as I wondered what the truth was. Did Rachel know that

Quinton killed my mom? Was that why she didn't want me to go home that night?

With my head in a whirl and my heart broken, I jerked my hand from Quinton's grasp as tears burned my eyes. How could he?

"Justice..." He turned to look at me and I could tell in his eyes that he was guilty of something. "Let's go!"

"No! I'm not going anywhere until the two of you tell me what you've been hiding! Ever since that night my mom died, you have been trying to keep me from talking to Rachel! And ever since that night, I felt as if you have been keeping something from me! Did y'all work together to kill my mom?" I asked. "Rachel did you know?"

"WHAT?!!" Rachel asked as she shot Quinton a disgusted look. "What's she talking about?"

Surprisingly, she looked genuinely shocked by my question. Right away, I could tell that she had no idea what I was talking about.

"Justice, I don't know what the fuck she's talking about! Baby, I already told you that I didn't have shit to do with Val's death!" Quinton stated as he stared into my eyes.

"Then what are you two hiding from me? And please don't tell me nothing or try to get me up outta here because I'm not leaving until I..."

"WE'RE LOVERS!" Rachel blurted.

"Wh-wh-what?" I asked as I felt the room spinning.

"NO, we ain't!" Quinton denied.

"Quinton is it true?" I asked in a voice that was barely above a whisper.

"HELL NAW! I AIN'T FUCKIN' THAT GIRL!!"

As I looked back at Rachel, I saw that her eyes were filled with tears. At the same time, they were also full of love as she looked at my husband. This was all too much!

"That's what we've been hiding sis. I love him! I thought when he moved me in here that we'd finally be together... but then he went and married you!" Rachel explained as tears erupted from her eyes. "That's it! That's our secret. I'm sorry I didn't tell you sooner, but I tried! I honestly did!"

The amount of deception caused my head to spin until I became lightheaded. As my eyes rolled to the back of my head, I felt my body grow limp and collapse.

Next, the room went black...

To be continued...

Made in United States
North Haven, CT
14 March 2023

34060093R00114